Dogged
Determination

by

Chris Redding

The Wild Rose Press, Inc.
PO Box 708
Adams Basin, NY 14410-0708
Visit us at www.thewildrosepress.com

Publishing History
First Edition, 2025
Trade Paperback ISBN 978-1-5092-6236-6
Digital ISBN 978-1-5092-6237-3

Published in the United States of America

Dedication

To Noir

Chapter One

The planet does not have enough hair color to cover my white trash roots.

Daria Jacks's black pump tripped down the long, elegant staircase of the hotel ballroom in New Jersey.

White tablecloths adorned the round tables. White flowers sat in baskets in the middle of those tables.

The shoe clicked and clacked its way to the bottom of the marble steps. She gripped the cold, marble railing, warmth seeping up her neck.

Outclassed once again, she let her gaze flow over a ballroom filled with people who'd been born into money. A sigh escaped her lips. She shouldn't have been surprised she committed a faux pas this early in the evening. She locked her knees, resisting the urge to take a step.

She worked as a veterinarian in a small town in New Jersey and a good one. Attending a ball was not in her wheelhouse, but she did it for the animals and the no-kill shelter she wanted to build. Helping animals was all she'd ever wanted to do, and she'd dressed to accomplish that task.

Samuel Lafayette looked dapper in his black suit, with every brown hair on his head in place. He rolled his brown eyes. "Daria."

She shrugged.

Her date shouldn't expect any less.

At least no reporters were at this event. No one could record her gaffe for posterity.

More importantly, no one could ask her about her newfound father. She was done answering those questions.

Opting for a demure stance, she didn't chase after the footwear. Instead, as if no one could see she was only wearing just one shoe, she held her spine straight, facing forward. She pretended she hadn't been the kid with skinned knees for every major event in her life, except her birth. Each school picture sported a bandage on some part of her face.

If a hunky man in a tuxedo hadn't caught her footwear, then her errant shoe would have gone farther afield.

She grimaced at the idea she had a witness, other than her date, to her clumsiness.

The catcher had the blackest hair she'd ever seen. And the bearing of a Jersey Italian guy, sure of himself, but he probably had a heart of gold.

As he glanced up, a lopsided grin broke out on his face. He cocked his head and motioned to the shoe, his gray eyes sparkling.

She nodded and shrugged. As she battled the urge to swing her unclad foot, she couldn't deny the pump was hers. She remembered her dilemma, making her heart skip a beat. She'd sworn off hunky men.

And since he was at this ball, he was rich.

She'd sworn off rich, hunky men. Samuel groaned.

As she'd forgotten he was there, the sound startled her.

"I'll get your shoe," he said, his words coming out between clenched teeth.

No one in the expansive, chandeliered ballroom had seen her, so Daria didn't understand why her gaffe was such a big deal. She didn't make a scene on purpose.

Besides, he should be used to her by now. They'd been friends for years.

Samuel retrieved her footwear, the lights from the chandeliers glinting off his blond hair.

She smiled at passersby, not acknowledging her lack of a shoe nor backing down. She refused to show her fear of not fitting in.

Samuel and the shoe-catcher exchanged a few words.

The man smiled.

Unable to look away, she smiled back. Did she know him? Maybe he'd contributed to her cause at one point.

When he returned, Samuel was not smiling. "Here."

He put the shoe on her foot like a disgruntled Prince Charming to an incorrigible Cinderella.

Daria had no delusions Samuel was her Prince Charming. No, he was her way to raise money for her animal shelter. She had the charisma, but he had the connections. His musky cologne tickled her nose.

He stood and held out his arm. "Didn't I tell you what brand to buy?"

She slid her arm into his, just in case her feet decided to come out from under her. No reason to risk a second faux pas. "Yes, but my choices were either those shoes or paying the electric bill."

Samuel raked his gaze over her, his face scrunched, and his brows drawn together. He blinked a few times.

He'd been born rich and had never had to worry about anything since.

"I'll buy them, and I'll be at your office tomorrow."

"You don't need to," she began.

He put up a hand. "I do. If we're playing parts, then you must be costumed properly."

Because Samuel knew this world, and she didn't, she sighed and let herself be led down the staircase…never to meet the man who rescued her shoe.

****

Paul Vincenzo stood at the bottom of the marble steps, gobsmacked.

Servers traipsed around him with trays laden with food.

Regally dressed women gave each other air kisses.

The woman he couldn't stop staring at wore that green dress as if she were doing it a favor. She was short, thin, and had the creamiest skin he'd ever seen.

Jeeves, his butler, used gobsmacked.

For the first time, Paul understood the meaning. He felt his heart race, and he clenched his hands against sudden itching. What would her shiny, red hair feel like in his hands? When her lips kissed his, would they be expert?

Servers tempted him with mouthwatering appetizers.

Nothing would satisfy him until he knew her name.

While her shoe traveled down the steps, she held herself as if her shoe leaving her foot had been her plan, and she'd meant for her footwear to go first. Then the color rose on her cheeks.

He felt his heart stop for a moment.

When she smiled, her eyes lit up.

Before he could react, her errant shoe was now back on her foot. Paul didn't want to stop the interaction, but he had nothing to say.

Her date led her away. Led her away like a misbehaved child instead of the stunning woman she was.

He sighed. Why did the best women date men who didn't appreciate them?

Now, he had a mission—to learn the name of the most beautiful woman in the room.

****

No one had taken Daria's picture.

No one would discover who Dad was or where he currently resided. She could relax a little, and she let her shoulders down. At the table adorned with a centerpiece that was tall enough to block her view, she eyed everyone else's actions before she picked up her utensils. She'd been at many balls and fundraisers. Sadly, the information about what fork to use or when never stuck in her mind.

She had other talents than picking the correct utensil. One of which was separating rich men from their money for a good cause, of course, which was her animals.

"What do you do?" one of those rich men at the table asked her. He had a close-trimmed beard and tiny spectacles.

Now was her chance. The first question was always about your profession. "I'm a veterinarian."

"She also runs an amazing animal shelter," Samuel added.

Odd of him to be supportive.

The man cleared his throat. "Animal shelter?"

"A no-kill shelter," she began.

After each sentence, the man leaned closer.

He was hooked. She figured he'd be good for at least a few hundred. She would be a few more dollars closer to her goal of buying the property next to her office to build a bigger shelter.

The shoe-catcher sauntered by with a woman on his arm. He glanced her way. He sported a mustache and slicked-back hair.

Daria almost stumbled in her spiel.

He smiled.

No one should be allowed to be that attractive. She cleared her throat, then glanced away and back to the first rich man. "As I was saying."

The businessman shook his head. "Say no more. Here's my business card. Call my secretary."

****

"Where are the celebrities you promised?" Carmela Loschiavo asked.

She wore a green dress, and her olive skin was radiant, while looking around the ballroom with hazel eyes.

Paul should like her more than he did, but she was just a friend.

While she held a cocktail napkin of something mushroom, she hung on Paul's arm with one hand.

The earthiness of the food invaded his senses.

Most of the attendants had found their seats.

Paul had already placed Carmela's purse at their table. His blood hummed, and he doubted he could sit still just yet. Servers placed salads in front of everyone, so he needed to settle at some point. "Just a slow one," she said.

He led her to the dance floor, but his mind was back on the redhead. Who could she be? He hadn't seen her before, but he'd been out of the fundraising circuit for a few months. Excitement circled through him at the prospect of meeting the woman.

"Pauly, are you even listening?"

"What did you say?" He never should have asked Carmela, but he didn't want to be here alone. Most knew about Dad's will, and he wanted to have some buffer against the snickers. Dad was having the last laugh.

He returned his attention back to Carmela. She wasn't "the one," but he knew she could dress high-end. Too bad he wasn't in love.

She had a mane of black hair, and her makeup highlighted her brown eyes. Today, she was doing him a favor.

He should treat her with the respect she deserved. He shoved thoughts of the redhead to the back of his mind. Two more hours before he could leave and take Carmela home. Until then, he'd show her a good time.

And, discreetly, he'd inquire about the redhead that he doubted he would stop thinking about.

****

"Who was the guy who caught my shoe?" Daria asked on the ride home. She'd taken off the offending footwear and crossed her legs pretzel-style on the still new-car-scented leather seats. Her dress itched, and she couldn't wait to get into pajamas. How did people wear stockings all day, every day? The hum of the tires filled the car.

Samuel shrugged, his face lit by the glow of the

dashboard lights. "I didn't really catch his name."

The stranger's face flitted into her mind. She shook the vision away. Hopefully, he wasn't a reporter. "Then what did you say?"

"Some comment about women and their issues. Guy talk."

She whipped her head in his direction. "That comment wasn't very nice. I depend on these people for my shelter."

Samuel pulled into Daria's driveway. "I didn't recognize him, so he probably isn't big money."

She lived in a cottage behind the building. It was a single story with a stoop instead of a porch. She'd painted the shutters a happy blue. Easy commuting. "I do appreciate you jumping in and mentioning my shelter."

Samuel turned, and he flashed his perfect teeth. "We work well together. You know I hate to go to these things alone."

"We do." They had a friendship, nothing else, but lately, Daria had longed for more. Too bad her only social life was fundraising. Though a rich man could solve her money problems, she had no intention of dating a rich man.

****

Paul found Jeeves in the kitchen of the large house after looking everywhere else. Jeeves was his butler, a tall man with olive skin and an aquiline nose.

The mansion had twelve rooms just on this floor alone. This room had the best of every kitchen appliance on the market. The room was a monument to stainless steel.

He dropped his keys in a bowl by the door to the

garage. "Jeeves, I'm in love," Paul said, the emotion filling him with a sense of purpose. He had a name and a face, and he could find the address with Jeeves' help. Paul had floated home after dropping off Carmela. Now he danced into the kitchen. He paused with the garlic from his dinner still on his clothing.

Jeeves peered over his half-glasses at his employer, his green eyes sparkling. He sat at the giant island in the giant kitchen, a glass of wine and an open book in front of him. "Third time this week."

Paul undid his bowtie and dropped the paisley accessory onto the kitchen counter. He removed his gold cufflinks. They landed on the granite with a clink. Paul's mouth dried with the thought of the woman he'd sort of met.

Jeeves just didn't understand.

As if the heavens had shone a light just on her, her hair had glowed under the chandelier. He couldn't have stopped staring if he'd gone blind. "No. I met the most beautiful woman I've ever seen."

Jeeves put down his newspaper to sip from a glass of white wine. "I'll bite. Who is she? A Greek heiress slumming in New Jersey? No." Jeeves rolled his eyes. "A starlet on sabbatical."

Paul shook his head. He understood Jeeves's reluctance to believe him. Women had always been a salad bar, and Paul wanted to taste them all. This woman was different. "Jeeves, I'm serious. Her name is Daria Jacks." He liked the feel of her name in his mouth. *Daria.* He rolled her moniker over in his mind. What an interesting name.

"And what does this fine specimen of a woman do?"

Jeeves' question yanked him back to reality. Not many people at the event had even known her name, let alone where she'd come from. Like Cinderella at the prince's ball, she'd lost her shoe. "I think she's a doctor. Maybe a vet."

"You think?" Jeeves lifted his paper.

"I didn't actually get to talk to her." Paul had been a panther stalking his prey all night. She'd been seated well across the room. Her date hadn't led her onto the dance floor where he could cut in.

Her elusiveness made the chase even more exciting. His blood pumped, and he smiled. He straightened.

Jeeves frowned. "How do you know you're in love?"

"Something about her spoke to me. Something familiar." As if he'd known her all of his life. Or maybe in another life. He wasn't deep, but he just knew he'd made a connection; a meeting of the minds had occurred. Their psyches had bonded. He strolled to the fridge to pour himself some wine.

"Uh, huh."

Jeeves wasn't buying his story, but Paul didn't care. He had to meet Daria…as sure as he'd take his next breath.

"Pauly, you have a last request to fulfill. Focus. Don't go tilting toward windmills."

Paul eased onto the seat next to Jeeves. He put a hand on Jeeves' arm. "She isn't a windmill, Jeeves. She's *the one*. I can feel her in my bones."

Jeeves put his face back into his newspaper. "Bones? Your bones are not usually where you feel such things."

Paul chuckled. "She is different. Where's the phone book?"

Jeeves raised his eyebrows. "We have this thing called the Internet."

"Then where's my laptop?"

"Your kitchen one or our office one?"

Paul rose to find the computer. The first thing he'd do when he owned this house was to sell the monstrosity and find something more modern and manageable and in line with his style. "This place is too big."

"Don't mock the castle built by Vinny's Weenies. This place is your birthright," Jeeves called after him.

This mansion was Dad's taste. He shook his head. He could never bring a date or a wife here. Wife? Now, where had that thought come from? He located the computer before he booted up the machine and searched for vets. "Found her place."

"What?"

"Happy Valley Vet Clinic," Paul said. *Happy Valley*. Was that clinic where he was destined to find happiness?

Chapter Two

Two days later, Paul had put on a tie for the board meeting, but he knew that wouldn't last. He hadn't even tightened the tie fully.

Now, he sat at one end of a large conference table with ten men and women dressed the same way. The women didn't wear ties, but they were just as buttoned-up as the men. As if yearning for the wisdom of the world, the group chatted, and glanced at him. Their colognes mixed in his noise and made him want to sneeze.

Pictures of hot dogs adorned the walls. Couldn't they have come up with better things to hang on the cream-colored walls? The conference room reminded him of a menu on a shop down the shore.

What did he know? He was just the owner's son. Well, the deceased owner's son and poised to inherit the company when he completed his charity mission. He sighed and rubbed the back of his neck. Then he took a few deep breaths. Paul didn't want this company. He wanted to fix classic cars. Just like he'd been doing and making money for the last ten years.

Owners from all fifty states sought him out fix their pony cars.

He cleared his throat.

The whole room hushed.

They gave him the same respect they gave Dad,

which was nice. He hadn't earned their deference. "Thanks for coming today."

"We're sorry about your father," someone said.

He didn't know names or faces having only worked summers here. That was a few years ago.

They all murmured in agreement.

He was, too. The man was a son of a gun, but he was still Dad. And he hadn't wished the death he had on the old guy or to take over the company. "Thank you."

These people had liked Dad. He'd love to ask them why but chose not to. He had long ago reconciled the man who ran this company was a different man than the one who had raised him. "As you know, I haven't officially taken over the company, so I don't have any immediate plans to change anything."

He could hear their sighs, even if they were meant to be inaudible. He was an unknown quantity. "Dad loved this company, and he saw all of you as family. I really can't run this place. I'm a mechanic, as a lot of you know. I run my own business. Anyway, like I said, I haven't made any decisions. I want you to run the company as you have up until now."

"Your father told me that if he passed, we were to go to Ken Silverman, our Chief Financial Officer, until you stepped in," the man to the right said.

One of the vice presidents? Paul nodded. "I'm good with that."

"Do you have plans to sell the company?"

Paul tented his hands. The vultures had already begun circling. He'd received a generous offer just this morning. "I'll be honest. I've had offers. I'm not in a position to sell, but I promise if I do, everyone will be taken care of to the best of my ability."

He hoped. He didn't want to make that promise, but at this point, these people needed assurances. Their underlings needed to know if they had a job tomorrow. What did Dad see in his company? How could he hold the fate of all these people in his hands? He tugged at the tie which suddenly seemed much tighter. "Now, I know you have expansion plans," Paul said. "I'd like to hear about those."

****

As the metal door clanked behind her, Daria shuddered. That sound would haunt her forever. No matter how many times she visited her father in prison. After the lock was turned, she flinched. The stale air stalled in her lungs as she walked down the green hallway. The antiseptic smell assaulted her nose, but she guessed that fragrance was probably better than what the place could smell like.

Father. Also, the word took some getting used to. Her father was Mario Loschiavo. What little she knew of him was from the front page of the newspaper. He'd only appeared recently, and she didn't know how he fit.

And here she was visiting him in prison, where he was serving a sentence for tax evasion. Pausing, she gathered herself. She didn't want to bring negative energy. Butterflies flew around her stomach. No matter how many times she visited Mario, she didn't think the visit ever went smoothly. She padded down the hallway following the guard.

He opened the door to the visitation room.

Mario was already waiting. He looked up with dark, brown eyes and shy smile on his clean-shaven face. She slid into the chair across the table. Of course, she kicked the table leg, almost upending the plastic cup of coffee in front of him.

He sat behind a metal desk while the orange of the jumpsuit highlighting his olive skin. He studied her with brown eyes.

Since finding out about him just months ago, she visited him often but never grasped how Mom had once loved this criminal. Maybe he hadn't been a criminal then.

"Daria." He smiled and made to stand.

She waved her hands. "No hug."

"Not ready?"

She folded her hands in front of her. Their relationship was far too new. She just couldn't. "No. I might never be." She was also afraid she'd break the skinny old man she'd just met recently. While her pulse ratcheted up, she crossed and uncrossed her legs, wishing for a bottle of water to soothe her dry throat.

"You still mad?"

She searched her feelings. "No." Mom had kept him out of her life for a very good reason. She wanted to protect her daughter. At least she hoped. Since Mom died before Dad appeared, she'd never had a chance to ask her.

"What's new?"

They were still dancing around what topics to discuss. She wasn't good at small talk, but since she committed to visiting him, she didn't complain. "Same stuff. Still trying to build a shelter."

He leaned closer. "Daria, I have money."

She held up a hand. "We've had this conversation more than once."

"Dirty money. You think, at least. I made my

money legitimately. But you have your mother's scruples. You have that."

This argument was old, and talking it through again wore her down. "I do not want to discuss my plans again. I can build the shelter on my own. You will just have to assuage your guilt another way."

He coughed. "Your mother chose not to use her money, either. I have no guilt about how you grew up."

Mixed feelings danced through Daria. She had forgiven Mom mostly, but she still missed her. The three years she'd been gone had passed quickly. "Good. She did her best."

"But she never understood you," he said.

How did he know that information? "You my shrink now?" Did she get the snark from Mario? Or did he just bring out that trait?

Mario leaned his palms on the table. They were peasant hands with short, beefy fingers for such a skinny man. "No, but I'm probably the only person besides you who knew her. And I knew her as an adult longer than you did. She wasn't an easy person."

She cleared her throat, unsure if she wanted to know the answer to her next question. "I might regret asking this question. How did you meet?"

Mario shifted in his chair. "We met when my driver hit her car. She was so beautiful then. Confident."

Daria pondered his adjectives for Mom. Confidence was not how she'd describe Mom. When she knew her, she'd have a different boyfriend each month. Some moved in. Some just visited. "What went wrong?"

He frowned, and his eyes took on a faraway look.

"Hm. Probably me, Daria, dear. I thought I could protect her. I didn't protect her well enough."

"How so?"

He moved his mouth side to side. "She liked the glamour of the money. She didn't see the dark side until too late. Then she was pregnant with you."

"Is that the reason why she left you?" she asked.

"Probably. We never talked again."

"No?"

He glanced out the tiny window of the room. "She just left. I never found her."

"She was right under your nose."

He shrugged. "In a trailer park. Not using credit cards or the account I set up. Working menial jobs to make ends meet."

"She managed to hide."

****

Paul spent the next day in his garage, putting the finishing touches on a classic car but thinking about how he could contact Daria. He hummed as he worked. He had two bays and often had two projects going. As he'd been working on it for two years, he was excited to complete this one. When he finished with them, he placed tools back in their slots on the wall. Everything had a place.

He didn't own any animals, nor did Jeeves. Dad had not approved of animals. Could he buy one? Did they still have a pet store at the mall?

Later, as he showered off the day's work, Paul made a decision. He'd just approach her. No dog in tow, but him alone. Would that be creepy?

Paul Vincenzo. Well, Paul Vincenzo who was a mechanic and a working-class dog.

Most women were intimidated by the heir of a hot dog empire. That information could wait for a later date. He shuddered just thinking about the moniker he'd been given, Paul Gabagool Vincenzo the third. Way too much to give a girl to think about. Much too easy to turn him down.

Her shoes hadn't been the designer type the rest of the women wore, according to Carmela. No, he figured her for a simple, low-maintenance gal. Just what he needed. "I'll be back later, Jeeves." Paul exited the front door.

As Paul drove his latest beater car to Daria's office, the rain had begun pouring. He'd catch her at closing.

Something darted across the road in front of Paul's car.

He slammed on his brakes. He heard a thump, and a sick feeling pervaded his stomach.

****

Ready for her second fundraiser in a week, Daria traipsed through her back office to say goodnight to the animals. They were arranged in kennels along one wall with an examining table in the middle of the room under a bright light. Her last act was to turn off that light. With each good-bye she said, she was closer to the end of her day. She always finished the day this way, and the ritual gave her closure. Trudging out of the lab into her lobby, she spotted a black dog. "Where'd you come from?"

The hound and Labrador mix lifted his leg and peed on Daria's brand-new designer shoes.

She yelped and jumped away, but some of the liquid splashed on her anyway. Her blood pressure ratcheted up slightly. Now, she'd smell like dog pee.

She sighed and wondered if the dog's appearance was an omen for the evening. "Nice shot, pup."

The shoes were for Samuel. He'd insisted she needed to update her wardrobe. She should be more hip. As a teen, cool had been elusive enough. On the cusp of thirty, she had even less desire to attain that status.

The dog set down his rump and stared up with maple syrup eyes. His tongue hung out the side of his mouth. He had the head of a Labrador and the body of a hound.

How did he get into what was a locked office?

On the bright side, she could now wear sensible shoes. Samuel wouldn't want her to smell. She thrust her palms to her eyelids.

A tall man in ripped jeans and a black T-shirt a size too small appeared from around the reception desk. His black hair stood at odd angles from his head.

Did he own a comb?

"Dog," the man said.

His face was familiar, but she knew she'd never figure out where she knew him from. Her soul stirred. He reminded her of a stray who'd make a great pet with the right love and training. She shook herself. She saved dogs, not humans. Eyes as dark as molten chocolate took her in, then eyed at the dog. She jammed her hands into her armpits. "How'd you get in here?"

"The door was unlocked."

She narrowed her eyes.

He put up his hands. "Honest. It was."

She frowned. Her assistant, and best friend, had left the door unlocked again. In a rush to get home to her new husband. What would that situation feel like to want to leave work to be with someone? Maybe not her lot in life. She had decided a long time ago. The man's eyes were bloodshot, but her instincts told her he was okay.

The man gazed at the puddle and then her shoes.

She never should have bought these shoes, but Samuel had taken her to the store himself. At the memory of letting herself be bullied, she frowned. She possessed too much pride to let him pay for them. She'd eat boxed macaroni and cheese for the next two weeks.

He let out a gasp. "Oh. I'm sorry. He peed on you. Dog."

The dog just stared at the man like he had no idea who he was.

That was odd. Dogs stared at their owners as if they held the mysteries of the universe. In a dog's universe, they did. Maybe because he only called the animal *Dog*. Daria slipped off her shoes and padded to the reception desk for a towel. Glee lightened her step. Passive aggressive, she knew, but she picked her battles, and making Samuel angry would do her or her animals no good. Dropping the towel onto the puddle, she returned her attention to the animal in front of her. He showed no signs of neglect. "Is he yours?"

"No."

Explains the name. "Story?"

The man waved his hands. "He ran in front of my car. I almost hit him. I couldn't leave him out in the rain."

She glanced at her watch. The benefit began in fifteen minutes. She'd been cutting the time close before this distraction. The dog was cute, at least. She stared down for a moment before gathering herself.

The man hovered.

His closeness took her breath away. He was much taller than she was, and his presence was super-sized. She'd never been this aware of a man. She couldn't remember the last time that situation happened. "Let's start at the beginning, shall we? Office hours ended half an hour ago."

He put his hands on his hips. "I realize that. I just hoped someone was here. Dog's been throwing up."

Daria observed the dog's eyes. As she scratched him under the chin, she couldn't avoid him licking her face. "Did he eat something he shouldn't?"

The man's chuckle originated from deep in his throat.

Daria regarded the man's chocolate-brown eyes, so dark she could not see his pupils. "Your dog being sick is not funny."

"He's not mine, remember? I just found him on the road. When he got in my car, he threw up."

The dog rolled over, presenting his tummy.

"That's a good boy." She rubbed along his abdomen, feeling his ribs. "He's thin."

He didn't meet her gaze. "Uh, I guess."

Daria nodded. She couldn't turn away an animal in distress. Glancing at her watch, she stood. She'd be late, but her date wouldn't notice. He liked himself more than she liked him. He had his uses, and she guessed he had his uses, too. "You clean up his mess, and I'll take him into the exam room."

"Deal."

"Cleaning supplies are in the closet second door down the hall."

"Thanks."

His grin appeared from under a dark, black mustache. She shrugged and called for the dog, noting he didn't have a leash. "Here, Dog."

The dog's tongue still hung out the side of his mouth.

The expression on his face asked her to continue petting him. "I'll pet you when I'm done. Come on." The dog righted himself and followed her. She lifted him onto the exam table.

He licked her face. "Okay, Romeo. I need to check you out."

Chapter Three

As he cleaned up the dog's mess, Paul Vincenzo realized he hadn't even introduced himself. He slumped his shoulders and pressed his lips together. "Dang." The office had the kind of tile that couldn't stain and that made cleanup easier. The walls were a hospital green which made him wonder if that color was permanently on sale.

He'd been too dazzled by the green eyes and dark hair with a tease of red. She'd been too far away to see those eyes last night. The green sparkly dress was not what he expected the vet to be wearing. Guilt rushed through him, but he shrugged off the emotion. She could have declined or sent him to an animal emergency place. Guess her date could wait. He liked the idea her date last night wasn't important.

He returned the cleaning items, then strode down a hallway in the direction she had gone. He passed green doors set in even greener walls and spotless. He could probably eat off of the floors. He found her and the dog in an exam room.

While being examined, the dog once again flopped onto his back.

"I cleaned up."

She held up a long, slender finger before she put one end of the stethoscope against the dog's chest.

The dog gazed with the intensity a dog reserved for

someone with food in their hands. He wished someone saw him that way. Then again, Paul knew he hadn't done much in his life to inspire adoration. Wasn't a dog's love unconditional? Because they'd had no dogs in his house growing up except briefly, he didn't know for sure. Dad called them dirty beasts.

When she removed the stethoscope and slid that item over her neck, she glanced over her shoulder. "Can you take him home? I don't have room tonight. I'm expecting—well, I just don't have room." He rubbed a hand down his face. "You want me to take him home?"

"If you can. Otherwise, I'd have to see if another shelter will take him. And frankly, I don't like the other shelters in town."

What do I know about taking care of a dog? "Uh, okay. What do I feed him?"

"Rice and chicken?"

Paul wiped at his nose, and he wondered briefly if he was catching a cold. As discreetly as possible, he snorted. Did she expect him to take the dog home and cook a meal? He didn't cook very often. Jeeves made sure he ate on a regular basis. Did Jeeves like dogs?

"Yes, a bland diet. The food will settle his stomach. He probably ate something odd."

"Okay."

She nodded. "You should block him into a room like the kitchen or invest in a crate."

That seemed cruel. "I'm not putting my dog into a box."

"A crate isn't a box." She paused her hands on her hips. "Have you ever had a dog before?"

He shook his head, then he sneezed. "For about three days."

"Bless you. Buy a crate. Get him lots of toys to chew on. Dogs are den animals. He'll think of his crate as home."

Paul grimaced. "Are you sure that isn't cruel?"

"No, and the situation will be easier on everyone. He doesn't want to chew things, but he's bored. Are you gone all day?"

He waved his hand, not wanting to go into what he did for a living. "Not really. I do occasional work."

"Oh." She patted the dog, who stood, then jumped off the exam table. "I can give him shots if you want."

Dogs get shots? This situation was getting complicated. A sense of being overwhelmed cascaded through him. All he'd wanted was a date. Now he had a dog. A sick one, but a dog. "Sure."

"I don't recognize him as any of my patients. Maybe someone was passing through, and he got loose." She bent and scratched the dog's ears.

"Thanks, Doc. What do I owe you?" She still hadn't recognized him. He wondered if he should say something. His ego smarted, but then again, he wasn't in a tuxedo tonight.

"This time the visit is on the house."

He chuckled and then sneezed again. "You think there will be a next time?"

She smiled, and the gesture lit up her whole face and illuminating the freckles on her nose.

He was in love. He had to smile back.

****

Daria threw her car keys at the valet in front of the hotel in the small city forty minutes from her home. Many grand events were held here. She knew exactly which ballroom to find Samuel in. She wiped sweaty palms down her thighs. Having thrown the keys like someone who had never played sports, she caught the valet off guard.

Instead, the keys hit him in the head.

She stopped short, a hand over her mouth. "I'm so sorry."

The valet rubbed his head. "No harm, ma'am."

She rushed into the banquet room with her heart fluttering at being late, but she had no time for regrets. An orchestra played music in the corner, and the lights had already been dimmed for dinner service.

White-jacketed servers were just serving the salad.

Samuel Lafayette stood.

She wended her way through the tables on cheap shoes she put on instead of the new designer ones. Her feet thanked her. She'd toss the expensive ones into the back of her closet. Could they be cleaned? A glance around the ballroom told her the society page photographer was far away.

Two women, who were obviously sisters, stared. They didn't flinch under Daria's scrutiny.

"I'm sorry I'm late."

Samuel frowned, then replaced his expression with a smile. He kissed her cheek before sliding out her chair. "Glad you could make it. Vet emergency?"

Tearing her gaze from the two women, she barely registered the usual disdain in his voice. He never understood her concern for animals. If their partnership hadn't been successful, she'd have dumped him long before now. He was her entry into society to gather names for a future fundraiser. She was his date to functions his family expected him to attend.

Samuel seated himself.

A server put a salad in front of her.

She dove into her food that smelled amazing. Her last meal had been a veggie burger at noon.

"Pace yourself," Samuel said.

At moments like these, the reproach clear in his voice, she wondered if a kid from a trailer park ever fit into this world. Did she even want to? For the sake of the animals, she needed to pretend she fit in. She straightened, gazing around the table.

No one paid any attention. What was he worried about? "Do you know anyone here?"

"My boss is sitting two seats away on your left."

Now his attitude made sense. While she chewed the last bit of lettuce drenched in some odd, sweet salad dressing, Daria put down her fork. She wrinkled her nose, but she rubbed the skin back to normal.

"If you need to blow your nose, go to the ladies' room."

"Why are you so harsh tonight?" she asked.

He put a hand on her arm. "I'm sorry. I'm just a little nervous. I have my performance review tomorrow with that boss."

She straightened again while clearing her throat. The pressure was on. "Oh. I'll be on my best behavior, then." Not wanting to lie, she resisted the urge to promise not to wear her food. That promise wasn't something she could keep. She smiled at the occupants of the table. All the women wore dresses which cost more than her net worth, but she refused to be ashamed. Everything she owned she'd earned herself.

"Thanks," Samuel said.

A server took away the plates. Another replaced them with the main course.

While he ate the filet mignon, Samuel had ordered her some chicken. He'd forgotten again. She stopped a server. "Could I please have the vegetarian plate?"

The woman next to her put a hand on her arm. "You don't eat meat?"

Hoping to soften her answer, she smiled at the woman. "No, I don't." To Daria, the decision to go vegetarian had been a personal one. She didn't preach to others, nor did she care what other people did.

"No speech?"

The rest of the table stopped to stare.

Her cheeks warmed. She slipped her gaze away from the woman, hoping the conversation ended soon. She never questioned anyone else's beliefs; she didn't want to defend hers.

She put a hand on Daria's shoulder.

Everyone stared.

Daria compressed together her lips, as no doubt her complexion reddened further.

"I don't agree, but I respect your opinion."

The server took away the plate with the chicken.

Relief washed over her. The meat in close proximity had made her nauseous.

Samuel leaned closer. "You couldn't have eaten around the meat? You had to make a scene."

She clenched her hands in her lap. "The chicken was making me sick. Plus, I didn't make a scene." The tense moment passed.

The rest of the table returned to their conversations.

"Everyone was staring. That's a scene," Samuel said.

"Next time, remember to get the vegetarian choice for me." She resisted the urge to roll her eyes. The evening would be a long night.

One of the women who had been staring traipsed past the table, throwing her a glance.

Did I anger this woman somehow?

"Now your incorrect meal is my fault?

What was wrong with him tonight? "No, I'm making a suggestion. Boy, you're cranky."

Samuel shrugged, not arguing.

"Samuel," the man two seats away said. "Please introduce me to your date."

Samuel cleared his throat. "This is Daria. Daria, this is my boss, Wendell Calthorpe."

She pasted on a smile. "Nice to meet you, Wendell."

"Lovely to meet you, too."

She chatted with Samuel's boss and did her best to appear interested in stocks and bonds. Money bored her except when she was asking for donations. Those donations were the reason she was here tonight. "Can you point me in the direction of some potential donors?" she asked Samuel after his boss left to dance with his wife.

He frowned. "You're asking people for money?"

"I'll invite them to another benefit."

"Oh?"

"Yes, if I decide to hold one for my shelter."

Samuel rubbed a hand down his face. "Why?"

He asked that as if he had no idea why she attended fundraisers with him. "Why? Why does anyone hold a benefit? To gain money for a cause."

"They're just animals."

Her mouth dropped open. "Samuel Lafayette, I never knew you to be so cruel. You know how I feel about them." Where was the attitude coming from? He'd been supportive last night?

He put his hand on hers. "I'm sorry. I'm just tense tonight."

"You certainly are. Now send me in a direction before we have a fight." She leaned into him. "I could make another scene."

Chapter Four

"This is Daria. Leave a message at the beep."

Paul frowned, and then he hit the disconnect button on his phone. He paced his apartment once, then again not sure what to do now. Because it made commuting easier, he lived over his garage. He could fit twenty of this place into the big house where Jeeves stayed. Here he'd put up pictures of his favorite cars. Dad disapproved of the artwork, but Paul was at home surrounded by automobiles. None of these things currently soothed him.

He gazed at the lethargic dog who he'd named Spike and knew something was wrong. Was he in over his head? He could feel a sneeze coming on. He didn't have time to be sick. He had a deadline to get his latest project done and out to auction.

The dog had thrown up the rice and chicken onto Paul's expensive carpeting. He'd opened all the windows. He didn't want to take the animal to the emergency vet. He wanted Dr. Jacks on several levels. Okay, he did want to see her again, which complicated his plan to leave the dog. He had no room in his life for an animal.

Spike stared with sad eyes.

His whine blazed a path through Paul's heart. "I'll try again, sport."

The dog had liked her, so Paul trusted Daria, too.

Besides, she was gorgeous, which was reason enough to see her again. He dialed the number her service had reluctantly given him.

"Hello?"

Orchestra music played in the background. "Dr. Jacks?"

"Let me get into the hallway," she said.

As she trekked to whatever hallway she was talking about as the phone rustled. The memory of her shimmery green dress danced across his mind and made his mouth dry. He tapped his foot, taking in the limp dog. Would she remember him? Her not remembering him would be quite a blow to the ego. Since he'd been in her office, an hour had passed.

"Now I can hear you. Who am I speaking with?"

He ran a hand down his face, his heart thumping in his chest. "Paul Vincenzo. I brought in Spike earlier today. The little black dog."

She sighed. "How'd you get this number? Never mind. How is Spike?"

He had a certain charm, and he'd brought it on. Daria didn't need to know that information yet.

"He's throwing up again, and he's not jumping around anymore."

She sighed again. "Did you give him the rice and chicken? Nothing else?"

"No, that's all now on my carpet."

****

"I have to go," Daria said to Samuel after she found him.

He'd been at the bar, and he listened as he swirled an amber liquid in his highball glass. He frowned, causing lines on his forehead. "What?"

She reached into her clutch for her ticket for the valet. "I have an emergency."

Samuel frowned. "Isn't that what Animerge is for?"

She didn't want an argument or his disapproval as much as he had a point that she would miss donors. "Special patient." She shook her head. She didn't want to explain her heart leaped at the idea of seeing Paul again. What was it about him? She'd been drawn to him. He hadn't hesitated in taking in the stray dog. He must have a good heart.

"They all are, aren't they? I warmed up a few people for you. You'll miss the chance to beg for money."

"Oh, Samuel." She put a hand on his face. "You can be so sweet. I'll have to contact them another time. Can you get business cards? I really need to go." She hesitated. Should she rush to save one dog and ruin a chance to save others? Shaking her head, she knew that tangible help was better than future help. She would attend other benefits to raise money, or she'd have her own.

Plus she couldn't turn down an animal in need. The decision made, she firmed her jaw. She wouldn't back down. Her animals were important, and right now Spike was her animal.

"Okay."

His frown told her he wasn't. She didn't have time to soothe his ego. He couldn't understand about animal emergencies.

She couldn't explain the situation. Running down the steps in front of the hotel, she almost tripped. She landed upright, but the heel of one shoe broke. "Damn.

Cheap shoes." She toed them off and stood on her stocking feet. Maybe Samuel had a point about good shoes.

She gave the valet her ticket and then waited in the cold drizzle. She shivered and hoped the car wasn't parked too far away. After what seemed like an eternity, Daria saw her car pull up. She shook his hand, slipping him some bills for his trouble. At least, she tried. She ended up dropping the bills.

He grabbed for the money.

In the same moment, she did, too. She hit him in the eye with her shoulder.

"Ouch."

She covered her mouth. "I'm sorry."

The parking guy managed to stay on his feet.

Daria landed on her butt in a puddle. *Another dress ruined.* "How about I let you get the money?"

****

The dog sat dry in the car.

Paul paced outside the vet office in the light rain.

Hopefully, the dog was not throwing up anymore. Spring had sprung, and the air smelled like wet leaves.

The office was a squat building with a curved, black roof like a barn in a rutted parking lot off a road that wasn't a highway, but a busy route north and south during rush hour. Since rush hour was over, the traffic remained sparse. A lone light burned inside the red barn which housed Happy Valley Veterinary Office.

The dog wasn't making him happy. His need to find a reputable charity wasn't thrilling him, either. He cursed Dad for that stipulation in his will. How would he find a place he could become involved in enough to decide that's where the donation should go? Dad still had control from the grave, and that irked Paul.

Nope. The one positive in his life was a woman only interested in his dog.

A lone car coughed into the lot. Despite the vehicle's disrepair, he'd have known a classic pony car anywhere. Too bad, she didn't keep the machine in good shape. He could give her an estimate, ensuring his working-class image. He shook his head. His attention should be on Spike. That's what Dad had wanted him to learn. Or, at least, that was what the will said.

The dog had been nothing but problems, but Paul had a job to do. His decisions affected his future and his business. Too much was at stake to fail now. As he drove him here, he just realized the dog's role in his plan. Maybe he wouldn't offload the dog just yet.

The gorgeous doctor disembarked still dressed for the evening except her shoes were slung over her wrist. She opened an umbrella and then strode toward the building, keys jangling.

He couldn't read her expression, but he expected she wasn't overly happy to have had her date cut short.

"Where's Spike?"

As if she made dog calls in a shimmering evening dress all the time, her tone remained even. Paul had to admit she was showing more patience for this dog than he was. Paul indicated his beat-up car. "I wanted him to stay dry."

She nodded.

Her smile told him she was impressed by his decision to keep the dog in the car.

"Get him while I change into scrubs."

Paul did as she asked.

Daria had transformed herself. Gone was the green

35

dress which highlighted her eyes. Instead, she wore plain surgical scrubs with small multi-colored dogs on them. Black sneakers had replaced the heels, and her fiery red hair was pulled back into a loose ponytail. Wisps of hair framed her creamy-skinned face.

His breath caught. He itched to brush away one of those wisps. Jeez, he was losing his cool. She wasn't any less beautiful, but now she reminded him of someone he'd seen in the supermarket whose cart he'd bump into "accidentally."

His energy gone from the trek from the car, Spike sat at his feet.

Paul gazed at the dog, wondering if the four-legged beast was his ticket to fortune and this lady in front of him. Guilt raced through him. This dog and this lady deserved better than his playboy ways. Then again, maybe he should change his ways.

"Please put him on the table."

Daria's voice interrupted his musings. Paul lifted Spike who was dead weight in his arms.

She listened to his heart and checked his eyes and ears. "I'll take some blood. You can't think of anything he ate that he shouldn't have?"

Paul searched his brain. The dog hadn't been anywhere near his garage. He couldn't have gotten into any fluids there. "None that I can think of."

"He'll have to stay overnight. How about you search for anything chewed and call the office early tomorrow morning." She took the dog off the table, then led him out of the exam room.

Paul followed her into a back room filled with cages. The walls were painted a utilitarian green. The pungent smell of many animals stung his nose. He sneezed twice.

"Bless you. Sounds like you've got a cold."

"I guess so," Paul said.

She placed Spike into a larger cage. Strolling past the rest, she stuck her finger to touch each animal and cooed.

A small, furry dog stared with soft brown eyes. Paul averted his gaze lest another animal worm his way into his heart. "Are all of these animals sick?" He never knew he had such a soft spot for the furballs.

Zeroing in a dog, she stopped. "No, some of these are strays up for adoption."

Her perfume danced around his nose. Not an expensive scent, but one which suited her. He didn't want this encounter to end. Daria was the first woman in a long time who held his interest. "This place is a shelter?"

"And a vet office. The vet office partly funds the shelter."

"Partly? What else funds your shelter?"

As she led him back to the lobby, she chuckled. "Mostly me begging."

"Maybe I can help?"

She looked him up and down.

He knew her picture of him, and he agreed he dressed like a slob. Maybe an unconscious way to avoid the money issue was to dress as if you didn't have any. She'd bought the impression he'd wanted to give.

But he could help her without her ever knowing. This plan was how his father had wanted Paul's inheritance to be. With no accolades or recognition. Just volunteer at the charity, then give the money.

"How?"

His ripped shirt didn't reflect his potential bank account, and he liked things that way. Dad had warned him about gold diggers from a young age. "Don't let appearances fool you."

She stiffened. "Sometimes appearances are all we have."

A rumble emanated from her stomach. Paul realized she must have missed dinner. An idea struck him. "Let me buy you dinner." He'd revisit the money issue later more subtly, so she'd never think of him as the donor.

She glanced out at the raindrops racing each other down the window. Something barked, and she opened her cell phone. "Jacks."

He shuffled a few steps away.

She argued with someone. Her face reddened, and her words became clipped. She shut off her phone and then stared out the window again.

"Problem?" Paul asked.

She shook herself and then she smiled. "Nothing I can't handle." She snapped her fingers. "I better run one of those blood tests tonight in case what's wrong with him is what I think it is."

Concern marched through him. "What do you think is wrong?"

"Antifreeze poisoning."

He squinted. "Is that bad?"

"The worst. Without treatment, he could die."

Chapter Five

Despite not showing the dog much affection, the man did care about Spike. Maybe Paul wasn't a demonstrative person. Who was Daria to judge? At least he'd brought the animal in to be seen. They stood in her green-painted exam room. As she studied the walls, she wondered if she could have chosen a better color.

Shaking herself, she went back to her perusal of Spike's owner. Daria didn't trust anyone who didn't like animals. Samuel, at least, had a cat. He just never appreciated her animals taking her away. "I have to send the results out to a lab. I can pull some strings to get the test done first thing."

He frowned. "There isn't someplace to do the test tonight?"

She had to admire his concern for the dog. An attractive guy who loved animals couldn't be all bad. He probably wasn't rich either. That was a plus in her book. "No, no one's open." She dropped the test tube into a mailer. She missed.

The man caught the vial before the glass tube could shatter on the floor.

She took it and then placed the tube into the mailer. "Thanks."

"You're welcome. Let's get some dinner."

The rumble from her stomach could have

awakened the dead. "I don't think so."

He cocked his head. "You're hungry. I'm hungry. I made you miss your dinner."

Her mouth dropped open. Even though the event had been on her mind all week, she hadn't remembered the benefit. Something about this man made her mind go blank. What was distracting about him? Was she distracted by the way he gave her his whole attention? She'd missed a great opportunity to network with rich people. "Trust me, we will bill you."

He grimaced and waved his hand. "I know. I'm trying to make your lack of dinner up to you personally. We could get a burger at the diner down the road." He raked his gaze over her.

She glanced down. She'd picked stained scrubs, and now, the outfit had black hair from his dog. "I'm not dressed for going out."

"The diner doesn't care."

He had a point. People from the local hospital often ate there in their scrubs. No one would bat an eye.

She was hungry, and her refrigerator was empty. She cursed herself for not getting to the grocery store at lunchtime. Another animal emergency had kept her here, consuming someone's diet shake. Puppy-like eyes stared back.

She sighed. What could a meal together hurt?

****

Paul said his good-bye to Spike whose posture reminded him of pouting, even though he knew dogs couldn't make expressions like that. "I'll see you in the morning, Spike."

Spike spun away and settled on the bed at the back of the cage with his butt toward Paul.

Even with his limited experience with animals, Paul knew he'd been dismissed. "Fine." Paul leaned against the reception counter, the lobby slightly more colorful than the rest of the place. Someone had hung a wallpaper border of cats and dogs near the ceiling. He rolled her name around in his mind for a few minutes. He'd never met anyone with that name and liked it. He grabbed a tissue to blow his running nose.

She appeared from the back. "Ready?"

Her hair was tied back neater, and she'd changed into different scrubs. These had cats on them, but they didn't enhance her figure any more than the other ones did. Shame, but he couldn't be too picky. He'd seen her in a dress. He knew a bit about what was underneath those scrubs, and his imagination could conjure the rest. A nice set of legs had come out of that sparkly dress. Too bad, she hid them now. "I'll drive."

She nodded. "Let me lock up."

The rain had stopped, but the night had cooled. No stars shone in the sky, but Paul glanced that way anyway, then went back to Daria. "You have a coat?"

She returned with a deep burgundy raincoat.

He helped her with her coat. He opened the car door.

She slid onto the seat, only hesitating once.

Because of the dog, he'd taken his beat-up car. His nice car had leather, which was easier to clean, but he'd opted for cloth seats. Thankfully, Spike didn't throw up during the whole trip.

"Is Spike your first experience with a dog?"

He started the engine, praying the motor turned over. "As an adult. I had a beagle for a few months as a kid." Mom had bought him one to defy Dad. The man had returned from a trip, and the dog was gone two hours later. He'd forgotten about that dog until now.

"A few months?"

Paul cringed at the story. The dog had been a pawn in a power play that didn't make either of his parents look good. "Dad made me get rid of the dog. He didn't like the mess."

She shifted to look at him. "Shame. Where did you put the dog?"

He pulled out of the parking lot. "A relative adopted him. He ended up living on a farm, and I could visit him once in a while."

"That's not so bad."

Paul slid into a spot right by the door of the diner in case rain fell on their way out. The eatery was a vintage New Jersey diner. Metal wrapped around the outside. Inside, booths lined one wall. A counter with round, red seats paralleled the open kitchen. He held open the door.

While the aroma of meatloaf wafted toward them, silverware clinked. A large glass-covered dish held pie.

With the dinner rush over and the after-bar crowd several hours away, a few customers occupied the counter.

Daria picked a booth.

Paul slid in across from her. He'd stopped sniffling and sneezing.

The server and the cook in the kitchen bantered.

When she snagged the menu, she knocked over the salt shaker.

Paul grabbed a napkin.

She took the paper, gathering the salt together, and brushed the crystals onto the napkin.

The server appeared in a polyester uniform with a stained apron around her soft middle. "What'll you have?"

Paul indicated she should go first.

She shook her head. "I'm not ready."

"I'll take the diner burger. Do you have whole wheat buns?"

The server grunted.

Paul took the sound for a *yes.* "Then I want the whole wheat bun. May I have a vegetable instead of the fries?"

"Honey, I can get you some veggies, but the cook's been making burgers with fries for years. He'll put them on the plate, no matter what I say."

"I'll have the fries."

The server shrugged.

"Can I have the Greek salad, please?" Daria said. "No onions. Dressing on the side."

With the order taking done, the server waddled away.

"You eat meat," Daria said.

He leaned back in his seat, having never been asked that question before now. "Yes."

"Have you ever considered becoming a vegetarian?"

Paul shook his head. "No. Never. Do you feed the dogs meat?"

She blinked. "Of course. Dogs are carnivores. They're built that way. They need meat."

"Then I'm a carnivore. I have no choice."

She jiggled her head and laughed. "I don't agree, but I'll drop the subject."

"Then let's agree to disagree." He hoped his grin

smoothed over the situation. He knew he was on shaky ground here. Meat and potatoes were a staple. Jeeves had tried to expand his palate, to no avail. And what would she think about how Dad made his fortune?

****

Daria answered her phone, turning in her seat. No one occupied the booth behind her, and she didn't want to go out into the drizzle. If she stayed put, she wouldn't disturb anyone. "Hey, Samuel." The squeak of the vinyl seat made her smile for a moment. They'd argued before she left the benefit. Was he making up?

"Where are you? I stopped by your place. I got a doggie bag of food," Samuel said.

She smiled. "Thanks, I'm out having dinner." When he wanted, he could be thoughtful. He was trying to make up.

"Where? I'll join you."

Her breath left her for a moment. He couldn't show up here. Besides, she'd have to explain to Paul. And she couldn't. Then she relaxed. "Uh, no. I'm almost done," she said. "I'm in a diner." Samuel didn't set foot in diners.

"Okay."

She let out a breath, expecting him to argue. "I'll call you over the weekend." She disconnected.

The server delivered their plates.

Paul didn't touch his food until she picked up her fork.

"Sorry, I don't like answering during a meal, but I wanted to make sure this call wasn't an emergency."

"Didn't sound like it." He took a fry off his plate, offering her the fried potato.

She declined. She drizzled the dressing over her

bowl of greens. She dipped her fork into the small dressing container, which she knocked over.

The stream raced toward Paul. He used his napkin to stanch the flow.

She wanted the earth the swallow her. Even if she didn't have romantic notions, she didn't want to make a fool of herself. "I'm sorry. I'm a little clumsy."

He shrugged and dove into his burger. The juice from the meat ran down his fingers.

The rivulets reminded Daria of something she didn't want to remember. She stared, scrunching her nose and drawing together her eyebrows.

"Boyfriend?" he asked.

"Hm?"

"The phone call?"

Samuel was none of Paul's business. "Friend."

"You didn't tell him you were with someone."

She waved a hand in the air. What was between her and Samuel was simple, but complicated to others. They certainly didn't love each other. She didn't expect Paul to understand this relationship. Men could be territorial. "We aren't like that. What is going on here isn't any of his business."

"Then no harm in telling him, then."

She wasn't going to argue. "I just didn't." Not sure of her own motives, she was happy after he changed the subject. Later, she'd have to figure out why she hadn't told Samuel.

Then her phone barked. *What now?*

Chapter Six

Daria glanced at her phone and slid out of the booth. "I'm gonna take this one outside."

"Okay." Paul stared out the window.

Silverware clinked, and the cook in the open kitchen called out orders. As he watched her, the noise of the place receded. How did that happen?

Daria paced in and out of the parking lot light closest to where he sat. Her ponytail bounced. Her brow was knit, but she listened.

Her intensity gave him pause. Paul wasn't that serious about anything.

When she switched off the phone, she looked off into the distance. Then she set her mouth in a firm line and marched back inside.

He doubted he'd like what she said next.

She didn't look directly at him. "I have to go."

He glanced at her plate, then her exhausted eyes. "You need to finish." He didn't want the evening to end. Maybe he was selfish to think that.

She frowned. "I ate most of the meal. Besides, losing a few pounds wouldn't hurt."

If she cut her hair, she might lose a few, but he didn't see where else she could lose weight. She wasn't a waif, but she had enough of her to hang onto. "Don't."

"What?"

46

"Don't complain about your weight. You look beautiful."

She shook her head and rolled her eyes, then shrugged. "Thanks for dinner. I'll let you know when I get the results of that blood test on Spike." She strode away.

Her exit took his heart with her. How had that happened this quickly? He dropped bills on the table, grabbed her purse, and followed. He caught up at the exit. "You're forgetting something."

She whirled. "What?" As she spun, she knocked her purse out of his hands which landed with a thud between them. She grasped at her bag.

But Paul grabbed for it at the same time, nearly missing his head with hers.

She stood.

That had been a close call. A concussion would slow his progress. He held up his hands. "Let me."

She grinned, and red appeared on her neck. "Thanks." She put the purse strap over her shoulder.

"Plus, I drove you here."

"Oh, right." She tucked an errant hair behind her head, a faraway expression. "I'm sorry to disrupt your dinner then."

He smiled, putting a hand on her arm. "No problem. Where can I drop you?" She was already onto whatever problem had been dumped in her lap. Maybe he could help.

"Back at the office."

He steered her out the door, his hand on the small of her back. "Sure? I can take you wherever you need to go." Because he understood she might not want him to know where she lived, he wouldn't compel her more.

She shook her head. "No, that's okay."

The rain had started again, but the precipitation was just a cold mist. He unlocked her door.

She shivered.

He slid behind the wheel, started the car, then turned on the heat, full blast. "The heat will kick in in a minute."

Daria hugged herself. "It's not that cold, just really damp."

"Maybe you should put more clothes on before you go out again." He wanted to bite back those words. He shouldn't tell an independent woman like her what to do.

She looked down. "Not a bad idea. I'm not dressed for anything other than the office."

Because she hadn't taken his words the wrong way, Paul let out a sigh. He didn't want to insult Daria. She deserved much more than that. She deserved a man who was in her corner one hundred percent.

At the vet's office, a woman waited in the parking lot.

"Friend?"

"Best friend," she said. "Thanks for everything." She flashed him a half-hearted smile.

He took as a whole. He wasn't a man used to taking scraps. For her, he'd consider doing just that. Paul shut off the car. Where would two women be going late on a Friday night? They weren't dressed for a club. He climbed out of the car while smiling at the other woman. The woman's features were Roman. Her stiff spine and fisted hands didn't welcome him.

The tall blonde eyed him. "Who is this?"

As if they were on some clandestine mission, the

woman had sounded defensive. Was this trip a matter of national security? Had he stepped into a situation he'd regret?

"This is Paul. I don't remember your last name," Daria said.

"Paul Vincenzo. Nice to meet you." He held out his right hand.

The blonde took his hand after a moment. "Shelley Woods." She swiveled. "Is he coming with us?"

"No, he's just dropping me off." Daria strode to her car, keys ready.

He'd been dismissed. Too bad he wasn't dismissed so easily. Each time he peeled back a layer of her, he liked her more. She became more interesting with each reveal. Her engine made a dying cow noise. Probably her alternator.

"Damn," Daria said.

He stepped to where she sat. "Problem?"

"My car won't start." She gazed past him, a frown creasing her forehead. "Shelley, can we take one? Do we need both?"

Shelley frowned. "Nope, we need two. I've got the cages stacked in mine."

This night was getting more and more interesting. He wasn't ready to go home yet. Why not go for an adventure? "We'll take mine."

Daria eyed him. "I wouldn't want to impose."

He shrugged. "You aren't. This way, I don't go home to an empty house."

****

"We're going to Trenton," Daria said as he headed south on Route 1. Traffic was light, not the usual for this road. People were at home and not trying to get

49

there.

He shifted gears and turned on the radio. "What's in Trenton?"

She glanced his way. "A shelter."

"Homeless?"

Shaking her head, she answered, "Animal." She didn't expect him to be happy about the situation. He'd complained enough about Spike. This hour was also not the best time to be in Trenton, but they had no choice.

"And what are we doing there?"

Where did she start? "The animal control officers found a large group of dogs in an apartment. The owner died in the hospital with no living relatives. The landlord had been on vacation, and no one checked on them."

He nodded.

Why was he going along with the drive?

"What are we going to do with them?"

She stared out the windshield. "This shelter will euthanize most of them. We're saving them, so they can be adopted."

"Are you sure you have homes for them? What if they aren't adoptable?"

She crossed her arms, having encountered this argument before. She worked with the families to make sure the adoption was successful. "No animal is unadoptable. I have to find them the right home."

"So, what's Shelley's role in this situation?"

"She's one of the foster moms. If I don't have room, she takes in some animals. Mostly dogs, but some cats. She has a farm."

"Oh."

She didn't think he understood, but he was

humoring her. Daria regretted bringing Paul along.

Shelley had convinced her saving animals was a good cause.

At that point, Daria was already a vet. Shelley didn't have to work too hard on her. They'd been a dynamic duo since.

"We aren't stealing the animals, are we?"

She chuckled. "No, one of the animal control officers called Shelley to see if we could take some of the animals. He'd rather not kill them, but that's the policy of the shelter. It's a small place and can't handle too many dogs."

Paul drove on, nodding slowly.

She hoped he was digesting all of that information.

****

Daria's hand on his arm warmed him. He wished for a sweatshirt, but he'd gone off toward the windmill without one. But her warmth soothed him, and the scent of peaches filled his nose.

The dash lights in his cheap car didn't do her any justice, but she was more beautiful than she looked now.

Dad's words echoed in his brain. "Someday, you have to become more responsible. Think of other people besides yourself."

Shaking off the memory, he gazed at her for a moment. Her confidence overwhelmed him. Her drive exhausted him.

She was determined to save these animals. She was willing to go out on a rainy, cold night, in just her scrubs and a jacket to get them. Her commitment showed how important these animals were.

"What will we do when we get there?" He had no

desire to be alone with his thoughts. Was that why he chased the wind? He shook himself, not wanting to analyze his current course of action.

"Shelley has cages we have to put together. Apart, she can fit them in her wagon. With animals, we'll need your back seat." She put a hand to her mouth. "I never asked if that was okay. I'm sorry."

He laughed at her wide-eyed expression. "Only Spike's been in here, but I don't think the upholstery will be ruined."

"What if one of them throws up?"

"A carsick dog?" Paul asked.

"Possible, not probable."

He shrugged. He'd committed, and he wasn't leaving these women stranded on a rainy night. "The seats are cloth. This vehicle isn't my best car."

She gazed around the interior. She squeezed her lips together. She shook her head. "You have another car?"

"Several." Going down that road might lead to too many questions. He was slumming today. Daria didn't need to know that. "How many dogs?"

"Maybe five. Four small and one large. The small ones will fit in the cages. The large we have to convince them we can handle without him being in a crate," she said with the seriousness of a general doing battle.

"Do you have room for them at your place?" he asked.

"Between me and Shelley, yes. Just. We can't take anymore, unfortunately." She twisted in her seat. "They might not be in great shape. I hope you aren't squeamish."

His squeamish level had risen every time Spike had

thrown up on his carpet. "I think I'll be fine."

"Good."

Paul cleared his throat. This trip was an adventure, but not like anything he'd ever done before. "Are you having second thoughts about me coming?"

"Yes, I've never asked anyone, but Shelley, and you're really a stranger."

He cocked his head. "Hardly, we've had dinner together."

"A dinner that was interrupted. I'll have to make it up to you."

The idea warmed him. "I'll have to let you."

A small smile broke out on her tense face. Then she gazed out the window. "Turn here." She said the direction all of a sudden.

He reacted without thinking. A lesser driver would have put the car on two wheels. He wasn't a lesser driver, having raced more than once. He missed those days.

"Sorry, I should have told you sooner. Trenton has many one-way streets that we'd have to drive several blocks out of our way if we missed a turn."

This night would be fun as his adrenaline began to flow. "No problem."

"The shelter is on the right. Park behind Shelley's car."

He did and put on his emergency flashers.

She climbed out. "Wait here."

He pocketed the key and then followed her.

She glanced his way.

Once again, his chivalrous nature had reared its head. This place wasn't in a nice neighborhood, and two women alone would get approached. His presence would deter them.

"Officer Graney is still here, but not for long. We need to hurry," Shelley said from the doorway.

Daria spun. "Can you put the cages together?"

He saluted and pulled out two parts of what must be the cage she was talking about.

The two women disappeared into the building.

He scoped out the neighborhood, wondering if even his beat-up car was prime for stealing. The wreck could be used for parts. The containers came together with ease. He lounged against Shelley's station wagon.

A door opened, and Daria motioned. "Bring in two crates."

He grabbed two of the containers. After closing the hatch on the wagon, he walked to the building He glanced up and down the dark street one more time. Some of the streetlights were out.

By the time he entered the building, he no longer saw Daria. In front of him was a hallway with doors off either side. Some were open while some were closed. He knew enough to move forward, but how far? "Doc?"

"Back here."

He followed her voice and the smell of urine, dog and cat, he presumed, hit his nose. He sneezed.

"Are you allergic?" Daria asked, her brows together.

"The scent of pee is overpowering."

The two women exchanged glances.

"We don't notice the smell anymore," Daria said.

"Lucky you."

Daria slid a white ball of matted fur into one of the containers. Then she put another multi-colored dog into the second one. "Put one in Shelley's car and one in yours."

He did and returned with another container. "Some guys are hanging out there. Don't go outside without me."

Daria waved a hand. "We'll be fine."

"No, you won't," he said.

Shelley relieved him of the other two containers. She filled them and then she handed them back. "One in my car, one in yours."

Daria followed him. Opening the door, he searched for the three guys who had been in the doorway across the street. He didn't see them nor did he see his car. The vehicle was just a mid-sized sedan, but the car had been his first. He'd fixed it from almost a shell. The loss pained him.

Her breath hitched from behind him. "Oh, no."

"My car's gone." He liked that car, and he'd paid off the loan a million years ago. He sighed. Time to find another beat-up one he could take anywhere. He'd miss that car, but such was life. The car was a write-off.

"Oh, my goodness." Shelley stepped out onto the street. "The car's gone. The dog's gone with it."

Paul recognized familiar taillights at the end of the block. "There they are."

Shelley stared at Daria.

She, in turn, looked to Paul. "I'm so sorry, Paul. I'm sure the shelter will let us use their phone."

Paul shrugged. "Who are we gonna call? That car will be stripped for parts by the time the police get here."

"We can fit in my car. We'll have to squeeze. But we have to find that dog." Shelley motioned down the street where the car had disappeared.

As he loaded what he could into Shelley's car, he felt a sense of urgency. He could still see the car racing, as fast as that little car could go, straight away from them. "We'll be cozy."

"Now for Brutus," Shelley said.

That's when Paul noticed the Great Dane on the leash Daria held. How did he not see the dog that probably outweighed him? The dog might fit in the car if the humans didn't sit inside. "Uh, where is he sitting?"

"Up front," Shelley said.

"Is he driving?"

The skepticism dripped from Daria's words. "Think cozy." Paul smiled, echoing his words from earlier.

Shelley started the car.

Daria handed Paul the leash, then slid into the car.

Paul climbed in beside her before he coaxed the dog onto their laps.

"Come on, boy," Daria said.

At her suggestion, the mighty dog leaped into the car, resting his head on Shelley's lap.

Paul was treated to his rump. "Lucky me."

Then Shelley pulled away from the curb in the rain on a Friday night.

"Make a U-turn. I saw them go that way." Paul pointed over his shoulder.

Chapter Seven

As they raced toward the car thieves in Shelley's car, Daria bit her lip. She wrung her hands, because many things could go wrong. At least traffic hadn't slowed them. "What if they're armed?"

"We have to save that dog," Shelley said.

She'd forgotten about the dog. This situation was all a little spontaneous. She'd have preferred to wait for the police. The cops were who was supposed to handle these things. Ordinary citizens didn't go off chasing criminals.

Paul spoke around the dog's tail. He sniffed and snorted. "They're turning."

At the last moment, Shelley cranked the wheel to the right. Her tires shrieked. Her car protested the treatment. "Darn them. I'm not losing that dog."

As if they realized they were being followed, the people in Paul's car accelerated.

"Can this car go any faster?" Paul asked.

"Not with this number of people," Shelley said.

They weren't gaining on the car. In fact, they were losing, and Shelley's car shook and rattled. The vehicle wouldn't hold together at this speed. "We need to slow down."

Paul put a hand on hers. "Things will be fine. We'll get the dog."

You'd think he did things like this trip every day.

She stared for a moment. She couldn't really see his expression in the dash lights.

He sneezed.

"Bless you." Maybe he did go on adventures in the middle of the night all the time. What did she know about this dark stranger? She knew his name and that he'd taken in a dog named Spike, and nothing else. A chill skittered down her spine. She shook her head, not sure everything would work out.

Then lights appeared behind them along with a siren.

"Oh, shoot." Shelley slowed and pulled to the side. "I really thought we'd get them."

"Let me do the talking," Paul said.

What could he possibly say? They were speeding. Any cop stopping them wouldn't care they were chasing car thieves. Or dog nappers. She rubbed a hand down her face.

Shelley rolled down her window.

The officer approached, his steps cautious. He didn't come right to the car. He shone his flashlight around the inside of the vehicle. "Evening, ma'am."

Daria held her breath. She'd never been stopped by a cop before and didn't know the protocol. She decided keeping her mouth shut was the best option.

"Evening, officer." Shelley's voice shook.

"Vinnie?" Paul spoke.

Daria pivoted back to Paul. Then she and Shelley turned to the policeman who'd stepped closer.

"Pauly?"

"Can I get out and talk to you, Vinnie?" He removed the dog's rump from his lap and grabbed the leash. "I'll let him stretch his legs."

When the dog's weight left her legs, relief swept through Daria. She wouldn't have complained about the weight, but the dog had been heavy. She rubbed her legs to get the circulation going again. Paul and the officer were clearly old friends. They embraced the way Italian men do. They spoke for a minute, but Daria could not hear. She was too afraid to get out.

Shelley drummed her fingers on the steering wheel. "I wish they'd hurry. Who knows where that dog is."

"The dog is fine. Worst case, they'll probably let him loose." She wasn't sure, but she wanted to be. "Besides, Paul's probably getting you out of a ticket."

"Humph," said Shelley.

After a few minutes, Paul slid back into the car without Brutus.

"Where's Brutus?" Daria asked.

"Vinnie's transporting him to the station. He put out an All Points Bulletin on my car, but he doesn't hold out much hope," Paul said.

"So, what do we do in the meantime?" Shelley asked.

Paul settled into his seat. "We follow Vinnie to the station and wait out the evening there."

"Are we under arrest?" She could call Samuel. He'd be livid, but he'd know a good lawyer. Would this story be in the papers? What impact would the arrest have on her practice and her ability to raise money? She clapped her hands over her ears to keep the thoughts from swirling out.

He'd put his hand on her shoulder. "No, we aren't under arrest, but he can't let us travel with all of these animals stuffed into one car."

"So, we wait for them to get your car back." Daria

nodded, thinking the plan made sense. Even if the situation didn't.

He chuckled. "That car won't be found in one piece. But they hope they can get the dog back."

He was losing his car because he had such a good heart to help out two strangers.

****

The precinct house was full of the people who populated the night. The place smelled of alcohol and pee. The scent reminded Paul of Daria's back room.

Daria stared straight forward, but once in a while, she glanced at the occupants of the other bench against the wall. When she did survey her surroundings, she widened her eyes and pressed her lips together.

Pauly guessed a veterinarian from Central New Jersey didn't often see the seamier side of life.

She perched on the edge of the seat.

He handed her a cup of coffee.

Daria bobbled the coffee but caught the cup.

Paul didn't wear any of the liquid.

She flashed him a nervous smile. "Sorry."

He'd been in precinct houses more than once with many cousins and friends being cops. He knew his way around and how to appear like he belonged there. "No problem."

Dad would not be proud. In his beat-up clothes, he didn't stand out.

In her scrubs, she did. She sat with her knees and lips together.

The lines around her mouth made her appear innocent, not fussy or old as he would have predicted. He found humor in her predicament, but Dad had attempted to raise a gentleman, so he remained quiet.

60

"Thank you."

She took the brew but didn't sip.

Shelley had stalked off to harass the desk sergeant and then call her husband.

"Do we know any more?" Daria asked.

Paul leaned against the wall. At least the drunk guy sprawled on the bench behind him wouldn't stare anymore. "No, but if we don't hear anything soon, we can catch another ride home."

"How? You know a taxi that'll take all the animals?"

"No, I have some resources."

She narrowed her eyes and curved her lips downward. "I could call someone." She didn't stand or even open her cell phone.

Defeat tinged her voice. She probably hadn't expected the night to end this way. He wanted to take away that tone. "Nah, I got this situation covered. Everything will be fine."

She compressed her lips. "You keep saying that. When the night ends in the police station, I wouldn't consider anything fine."

Shelley returned with a triumphant smile. "They've found the car and the dog."

He'd never expected them, too. "Yeah?"

"They're bringing the dog," Shelley said.

Paul figured his car was long gone.

****

As they drove back to the office in Shelley's car, Daria hoped for an uneventful ride. The car would smell like dog, maybe forever. They'd dropped Shelley off minutes ago but still had animals to transport to the office. They weren't packed in like sardines, but the resemblance was close. Their situation was legal, according to Paul's friend.

The skies opened, and the wipers couldn't keep up.

Daria had no idea how Paul had arranged things, but the animals were in with them. Silence surrounded them except for the rain drumming on the roof.

To make matters worse, one of the dogs developed the farts.

"Oh. My. Goodness," she said.

Because of the rain, they couldn't open the windows so, they all had to suffer.

Paul laughed. He chuckled.

The desire to laugh affected Daria, too. A giggle erupted out of her, and she couldn't stop herself. They were close to the office before she could stop.

The dogs slept the whole way.

When they had offloaded the ones which were to stay at Daria's, she set about checking them.

Paul lingered in the doorway.

He was a polite soul. He must want to run screaming from her presence. He'd been all over Trenton, and his car had been stolen. She'd even almost spilled coffee on him. How could he act like this night was all an adventure? What dangerous life had this man led? Her pulse was only just coming back to normal. "Paul, thank you. What will you do about a car?"

"I'll call a friend to drive me home."

She'd been so focused on the dogs, she'd forgotten about Paul's ride. "Oh, how rude of me. I can drop you somewhere."

They stood in one of the exam rooms.

He put up his hands. "You have your hands full. Besides, your car isn't working."

With a dog on the exam table, the Great Dane had decided to sit on her feet.

Paul laughed, pointing. "I think you made a friend."

"Be nice or I'll send him home with you."

He paled. She'd never seen someone go white that quickly.

You'd think he'd never owned a dog. "I'm just kidding," she said.

"Oh, right." His smile returned.

That expression arrived so easily on his face. The gesture lit up his eyes. She liked that smile. "How about I don't charge you for Spike's vet bill? Will that make up for your car?" She still could not believe the car had been stolen.

Paul was not upset.

She couldn't stop thinking about his car. How could someone be so cavalier with a possession?

Paul shook his head. "I'll pay the vet bill. Don't worry about the car." He excused himself to use his cell.

She could hear his voice, but she could not hear the words.

He returned with his smile intact. "A friend's picking me up."

"That must be some friend to drop whatever he's doing on a Friday night. Well, Saturday morning."

"He didn't have much going on."

She nodded, deciding she didn't need to know. Spike would get well. Paul would be out of her life.

Sooner since she'd been bad luck from the start. She sighed. Somehow, she drove away every eligible guy.

Chapter Eight

Paul's ride appeared ten minutes later. Of course, Jeeves had driven the English luxury car into the puddle-filled parking lot. Paul searched over his shoulder.

Daria was nowhere in sight.

If she knew who he really was, she would ask questions. He settled into the butter leather seats. He wasn't comfortable with Daria seeing him. "Hurry up."

"Pauly? Why are we in a hurry?" the man behind the wheel asked. "Have you robbed a bank?"

Jeeves didn't do as he asked, so Paul explained. "I don't want someone to see me in this car." Jeeves didn't do anything he didn't want to. Paul threw a glance again at the vet's office, but the front lights were off. Maybe Daria had gone out the back.

"You ashamed?"

He wanted to pull rank, but he knew Jeeves wouldn't ever stand for that behavior. The man didn't need this job. "Jeeves, just drive," Paul said through clenched teeth.

The man did as he was told.

Finally. Paul didn't know if he would survive the night. So much had happened, he was even more intrigued with Daria than before. When his pulse slowed, Paul realized his driver was in his pajamas. "I pulled you out of bed. I'm sorry, Jeeves. My beater car was stolen."

"I live to serve."

The sarcasm in his driver's words made Paul smile. Jeeves was a leftover., He was only one of two servants he had kept after Dad died. The old man had made sure Jeeves was taken care of, no matter what happened. Which meant even if Paul didn't live up to the promise in the will, Jeeves would be okay.

Paul would miss the man who was more like a father than his own, so he had no plans to mess up and lose him.

"If I may say, you are flushed and excited."

Paul nodded, his thoughts turning to the redhead back at the vet's office. "I've had an eventful night. I rescued a dog. Then I met this amazing vet, then she dragged me to Trenton to rescue more dogs. I had a Great Dane sitting on my lap, and his tail did not stop wagging. I think I have bruises."

"A dog? You touched an animal?"

Jeeves's smile became smug. Maybe he just hadn't had any experience with animals as an adult. "What? I know. I really don't like animals, but this thing was pitiful."

"And you didn't just drop the dog off at the vet. Hmm."

"What are you *hmming* about?"

"I think that vet must have really been amazing."

The raindrops drummed on the roof of the car.

Paul couldn't make out Jeeves' expression, but from knowing him for so long, he could guess how Jeeves would react. And his expression included an eye roll. "I said she was."

"Master Pauly, you fall in love on an hourly basis.

When you say someone is amazing that only means she made you forget about the last woman."

Paul crossed his arms, ready to defend himself, but he realized Jeeves wasn't wrong. As the wipers streaked across the windshield, he glanced out. "Maybe this will thing is making me change my perspective."

Jeeves made a noise.

Paul couldn't interpret it. "What?"

"I think that was the point of this exercise. So, what happens to the dog?"

Paul shrugged. "I'll pay the vet bill, then I guess Daria will find him a good home."

"Daria? This woman is the goddess in a vet's coat?"

That description of her was apt. She had a huge heart, and Paul wanted to be in her heart. "Yes, goddess. Red hair. Sparkling green eyes. Too bad she's so serious."

"Serious? And you aren't at all. Sounds like a match made in Heaven."

Paul grimaced. Some days he wished for less honesty from the man. Because Jeeves would call him in that situation, he couldn't lie.

After Dad died, Jeeves had been given free rein to call Paul out.

"I don't need you to list my bad traits."

Jeeves shook his head. "That would take longer than the ride home."

"Jeeves. Were you cheeky with Dad?"

A chuckle rumbled out. "No, but he paid my salary."

"Good point."

Paul laughed. He could never accuse him of being

a sycophant. What a refreshing change. If his life hadn't been full of people sucking up before his dad died, once the terms of the will were common knowledge, board members of charities all over the Garden State were calling him.

****

The next day, Shelley poked her head into Daria's office. "You have two visitors."

Shelley's tone sounded like she'd just made a grand announcement. People visited her all of the time. "How is that special?" Daria was knee-deep in paperwork and hadn't expected any customers. She didn't appreciate the interruption but knew animals had emergencies every day. She pushed away from her desk, hoping she could reconnect with her work when she sat back down.

"They are of the human variety."

Humans visiting her would be odd and did warrant some special treatment. "Oh. Do I know them?" That was a dumb question. Shelley didn't know everyone Daria knew.

Shelley smiled. "I don't think so."

She would have to see them then. Daria minimized what she was working on and then rose. Papers cluttered her desk, but the work would have to wait. "Well, if you're done, you can go for lunch."

"You sure you don't want me to stay?"

Daria shook her head, puzzled. "Do they appear dangerous?"

"Well, no, but you never know."

"You're more cynical than I am, Shelley," Daria said. "I'm sure I'll be fine." Now Daria was intrigued by who her visitors might be. When the situation involved animals, she trusted Shelley's instincts but found her friend and co-worker was less trusting of humans. Her radar wasn't as good, so Daria wasn't worried about two people in her lobby.

"Okay, but call me if you need me back sooner."

Daria took a deep breath, fortifying herself for whatever arrived on her lap. So much had these past few months. The addition of Paul this week had her on edge. And Mario. She wasn't sure her feelings for Mario. Even still. She didn't know where he fit. Daria shrugged off thoughts of Mario and Paul. She pasted on a smile to deal with the visitors in her lobby.

Maybe the people were a couple here to adopt a puppy. Sitting in the waiting room were two women, obviously sisters.

She knew them from somewhere. They both wore clothes which could have been designed for them. No blue-light specials for these girls. Daria's scrubs were from a discount place. She couldn't compete on their level with these women, but that wasn't important.

Daria brightened her smile. "Can I help you?"

The two women exchange a glance.

Daria realized she was in messy scrubs. She paled in comparison to these women. But she wouldn't let them know she was uncomfortable. She strode around the counter hand outstretched. She kicked a dog toy she hadn't seen.

As if protesting when the toy landed at the feet of the two women, the plastic newspaper squeaked.

Both women looked down.

But she couldn't read their expressions. *Great first impression.* "I'm Doctor Daria Jacks. Can I help you with something?"

The two women towered over her.

Daria looked from one to the other, wondering who would start the conversation. They'd come here for some reason.

The older one spoke. "We're Carmela and Maria Loschiavo."

The name didn't strike her at first. She searched her memory banks.

They stared. Then she realized these two women were Mario's other daughters. She took a step back, almost stumbling over another dog toy. "My sisters."

They didn't smile. They waited.

What were they expecting of her? They might have only just found out about her. Their father wasn't forthcoming about too many things. She had no idea what he'd told these two women. "Let's sit, and let that all sink in." She sat.

When the two women settled, Carmela spoke. "We came to introduce ourselves. Dad insisted. Not sure why."

That told Daria where she stood. They weren't happy she existed.

"Carmela, that's not polite." Maria swiveled back to Daria. "Sorry. We're a little shocked. Daddy only just told us about you."

Mario had said they didn't know about her, but he clearly changed his mind. Daria would have appreciated knowing the reveal ahead of time. "He mentioned you ladies, but I hadn't really thought about the situation. I'm still in shock about finding him." She hadn't tried to connect with them, and maybe she should have.

Carmela eyed her. "What are your intentions?"

Maria put a hand on hers. "Stop. Forgive Carmela.

69

She's been the oldest, and now she finds out she isn't."

Daria could understand why these women were shocked. She'd been when she'd found out about her parentage. Her brain had taken a few days to wrap around the idea of Mario. Of course, he had a family, but she hadn't been ready to see her found family. "I'm not sure what you were expecting, but I'm just getting to know Mario. Did he tell you? He didn't know about me until Mom died. I never knew who he was."

"And you aren't here for the money?" Carmela asked.

Daria sighed. Aren't these things always about money? "Money?" She guessed Mario was probably rich, but she hadn't considered that aspect. As far as Daria knew, the cash wasn't legally obtained. She didn't know what these women knew about Mario's dealings. Her role wasn't to enlighten them.

"Dad is very rich," Carmela said.

Daria spread her arms wide, indicating the veterinary practice. "Uh, I guess he is. I make my own living."

Carmela shook her head, her lips going sideways. "So you aren't here to get his money. You aren't suing him?"

Daria looked from one sister to another. Why would she sue Mario? "No, really, I'm not."

The sisters exchanged a glance. A smile broke out on their faces. "Then welcome to the family."

****

"Daria has a secret admirer," Shelley said in a singsong voice.

The waiting room was quiet for a change, and the buzzing of the old clock in the wall in her office was the only sound.

Shelley sat behind the desk, a computer in front of her.

Files lined the wall behind her just like any doctor's office.

Daria stared at the large bunch of red roses her assistant-receptionist-best friend pointed out. She wracked her brain for who could have sent them? Would a patient have done it? Of course, a patient had sent them. "Where did they come from?"

"Read the card."

She searched in the maze of greens and thorns and finally found the card. Of course, she pricked her fingers several times. Her wounds summed up how her day was going after the visit from Carmela and Maria.

"I know who the sender is."

"Did you read the card?"

"Don't have to. Anyone who puts up with a Great Dane on his lap on the first date."

Daria sighed. "We were not on a date. He made me miss dinner at the benefit last night, so we went to the diner." Though she hadn't expected to see him again, Paul had been a trouper. She didn't have results from Spike's bloodwork yet, which would give her a reason to call Paul. She shouldn't want a reason, but she did.

"The benefit. Samuel? How did the event go?"

As she struggled to pull out the small card from the florist's envelope, Daria frowned. The paper sliced through her thumb. "I didn't get a chance to schmooze. Paul called about his dog again." She read the card.

"From Paul?"

Daria studied the flowers. They were overkill for what they'd been through. The man lost his car. She should have sent him flowers. "Yes. He must have blown a week's wages on these flowers."

Shelley put her nose into the roses and took a long whiff. "Why do you say that?"

Daria frowned. "He's a mechanic. Has his own business. He can't be making much money. You saw how he dressed."

"Appearances can be deceiving."

Daria shook her head, pressing her lips. "No, he was very blue-collar."

Shelley cocked her head. "Is that bad?"

Daria crossed her arms. Shelley knew her better, but no matter. She wasn't dating anyone right now. Not even a charming mechanic. "His paycheck isn't anything. Can you find a vase for those?"

"They are in a vase," Shelley answered.

Daria noticed the crystal vase the flowers sat in. She'd bet her next paycheck the flowers cost in the hundreds of dollars. "Oh, thanks."

"You taking them into your office?"

Daria shook her head. "They won't fit."

Shelley touched her arm, a frown creasing her face. "Take them to your place."

"No, let's let everyone enjoy them."

Shelley motioned to the back where the animals were kept. "Is that black dog Paul's?"

"Yeah. He called him Spike. Big name for a medium dog."

She lit up. "He's a charmer."

"Paul?"

Shelley laughed. "No, the dog. Jeez. You have this Paul on the brain."

Daria bristled at the knowing smile on Shelley's

face. Her best friend was happily married for ten years now and was on a mission to find a mate for Daria. The vet didn't have any time or interest in anyone other than Samuel. He didn't ask anything other than to be a woman on his arm. Okay, maybe sometimes he told her how to dress, but he knew more of these things than she did. "Stop. He's just a patient's owner."

Shelley shook her head, her long hair swishing over her shoulders. "He bought you red roses."

"Whatever." Daria waved her hands in the air. "Can you call the lab and ask if they have the results of Spike's test?"

Shelley crossed her arms, frowning. "You've redirected me now, but I'll come back to this subject."

Daria escaped to the back area to check on Spike.

He'd kept down the little bit of food she'd left. He wagged his tail, but didn't stand.

"Daddy will be in to see you." She'd assumed he would. He hadn't mentioned any plans.

The door from the lobby swung open and slammed against the wall.

Shelley arrived breathless. "Someone's towing your car."

Chapter Nine

Paul pulled into the parking lot at the vet's office in time to see Daria arguing with a tow truck operator.

Her hair flew in all directions.

The truck raised the pony car onto the flatbed.

Her small form next to the burly tow truck driver made Paul want to chuckle. To Paul, the situation was like watching a Chihuahua arguing with a St. Bernard. One day with Daria and he was thinking in dog metaphors. Time to diffuse the situation.

"This vehicle is my car," she said.

The driver held his finger on a button. The flatbed returned to level with Daria's car on the back. "Look, lady. I don't know what the deal is, but talk to Paul Vincenzo."

"Paul?" Daria asked.

Paul was located behind her. "Yes."

She whirled.

Shelley looked ready for a battle.

The lines on Daria's forehead were now furrows. "What do you think you're doing?"

He was suddenly the enemy. "I'm taking your car to be fixed."

She stood nose to nose with him.

Since she was shorter than he was, she was nose to chest. Her eyes were on fire. He found that oddly attractive.

She put her hands on her hips. "I am perfectly capable of getting my car fixed. All on my own. I'm a big girl."

He studied all of her. She wasn't a girl by any stretch of the imagination. He cleared his throat. "I'm a mechanic, remember? I'm having the car towed to my garage. I'll fix your pony car today and have the vehicle back hopefully tonight."

She narrowed her eyes. "What's the catch? Are we bartering for services?"

He shook his head. "No. I just want to fix your car."

She waved her hands in the air. "Just like that. I'm supposed to trust you with my car."

"Can I get going?" the tow truck driver called over to Paul.

"Yes." Paul nodded.

Daria raised her hand in the air to stop him. "Not yet."

"What?" Paul asked.

The driver frowned but leaned against the truck to wait.

Paul didn't want to argue with Daria, but maybe he'd been heavy-handed in this situation. He'd wanted to avoid an argument, but they were having one, anyway.

"I don't let just anyone work on my car," Daria said.

He took a deep breath, calming himself. "Daria, from the looks of your car, you don't let anyone do work."

Her back stiffened.

He must have struck a nerve. How could he get out

of this situation? He was going under with no life raft in sight. In more ways than one, he could deal with the current situation.

"There's nothing wrong with my car. No rust and clean for the most part. No dents."

She listed what wasn't wrong with her car. She'd been in this conversation before. Maybe with someone else. "I went to Trenton with you last night. On a dreary Friday night and sat with a large dog on my lap on the way home. My car was stolen while I was helping you."

She crossed her arms. "Your point?"

He wanted to take her in his arms, but they weren't there yet. "My point is, I've earned some good guy brownie points. At least enough for you to trust me with your car."

"He does have a point, Dar." Shelley piped up.

Daria waved a hand. "Stay out of this." She looked back. "I want an estimate before any work is done."

That was fair. He could fudge the details, anyway, so she didn't know exactly how much he spent. He couldn't stand to see a classic pony car in this level of disrepair and refused to let price stand in his way of fixing it. "Agreed." He caught the scent of peaches again. Was the scent her hand lotion?

She cocked her head. "Nothing will be done without my express permission."

Paul held out his right hand. "Agreed."

Daria grasped his hand. "And I'm paying for all repairs."

Her skin was the softest he'd ever felt. "Just parts."

Daria shook her head. "I'm not taking charity."

No. Paul wasn't letting her win this argument. "I'm not giving charity. I'm doing you a favor. You'll have more money to give to the animals."

She frowned but shook his hand.

He'd won. The animals were her weakness, he realized. He made a mental note.

"Now, you want to see Spike?" she asked, her tone softer.

He had to think for a minute. Spike? That had been a name he'd grabbed out of the air. He wasn't attached to the name or the dog. Still, he should go see how the animal was. He would commit the name to memory. He didn't want Daria to think him cold. "Oh, of course."

"He's in better spirits." She led him into the vet office with one backward glance. "Shelley, did we get the results of the blood test?"

She settled behind the reception desk. "The test came back negative for antifreeze."

Paul followed Daria to the back where the cages were lined up. He greeted all the dogs from last night. A tickle ran through his nose, and he felt a sneeze coming on. "Hey, Spike."

The dog wagged his tail and then stood.

As if Paul held the secrets of the world, Spike blinked his maple-syrup eyes. Maybe the dog had gotten attached.

"That's a good sign. I'll get a leash, and you can take him for a walk behind the building," Daria said.

His house had a lot of land. Enough for a dog, but no room for the little mutt. No, he wouldn't take on a dog. Could he handle a dog? Maybe that was the first step in taking responsibility. He could be responsible for a pet.

Daria held out the end of the leash not attached to the dog.

The earnestness in her eyes had him rethinking the dog situation. Just a walk. Nothing more. "Come on, Spike."

As if he'd just been released from jail, the dog jumped out. The animal trotted alongside Paul as if he lumbered with him all the time.

Those maple-syrup eyes might melt him yet.

****

Watching Paul and Spike leave put a smile on Daria. She had to admit he cared for the dog, and that made points in her book. She shook herself. She didn't have a book. She didn't want a book. She didn't even own a library card to get a book to put points into and not even for Paul. She sat in her office daydreaming about a man she didn't want.

"Earth to Daria."

Shelley's voice startled Daria out of her thoughts. She glanced at her.

"He's cute."

Daria rested her chin on her right hand. "He has those eyes."

"Yes, he does."

"They look up at you and beg you to love him," Daria said.

Shelley smiled. "Nice buns, too."

Daria straightened and blinked "Who are you talking about?"

"Paul."

Daria waved a hand. "I was talking about Spike."

Shelley laughed. "And therein sits the problem. You need to spend more time with humans than with animals."

Humans were so much more complicated than

animals. Daria always had trouble navigating social situations. That was the reason she relied on Samuel so much. "Animals give unconditional love. What more could you ask for?"

"A husband. Children."

Daria waved away the suggestion. She would get out of her comfort zone to actually meet someone to date. Of course, her thoughts led her to Paul, but she shoved away that thought. "No time."

"Make time before it is too late."

She rolled her eyes. "I'm not fifty."

Shelley cocked her head. "No, but that age rolls around sooner than you think. He's got an eye for you."

She blinked at Shelley. "Who? Paul? I'm sure he looks at all the girls that way. Besides, I have Samuel, and he's everything a girl could want." Not that she was dating Samuel, but he was her excuse not to date. Maybe that was her problem. No, she just didn't have time to date.

"And he's stuffy."

She shrugged. "Yes, he is. Maybe."

"You wouldn't have to buy expensive shoes for a date with Paul."

Daria smiled. "Might be nice not to dress for a date. Have a beer and a veggie burger for a change." She heard the back door open and realized Paul had returned from walking the dog.

****

Mom had told Paul eavesdropping was wrong. In his house growing up, listening at doors was the way to find out what was going on. Eavesdropping was how he discovered Dad was sick. Listening when he shouldn't have been how he discovered Daria wanted a blue-collar guy, not somebody with lots of money. She wanted a solid, normal person. He stood in the back, straining his ears.

Too bad Shelley and Daria had ended their conversation.

He could be a normal person. He didn't have to take Dad's money, even if he completed the details of the will. That thought had not occurred to him. He tucked away that idea. But first, he had to ask Daria out on a date.

Her friend brushed past him as she left

Paul entered her office. He smiled at Daria, who was holding one of the small dogs they'd rescued.

She talked to the animal in a high voice reserved for puppies and babies. Rubbing the dog against her cheek, she called the beast cutesy names.

He should be skeeved, but he found her behavior endearing. Her love for the animals made her more attractive. "You truly care about the animals."

She parted her lips. "Of course." She put the dog back in the cage. "Did he go?"

"Pooped and peed."

"Good. I'll give him some more food. He might just have eaten something he shouldn't have. His stomach will settle."

Now or never, he decided. He had her alone, so he might as well make his pitch. "That's good. You free tonight?"

Her brows knit? "Free for what?"

Was he bumbling the invitation so badly she had no idea what he was asking? Had he lost his smooth touch?

"He wants a date." Shelley's voice traveled from

the other room.

Guess he wasn't the only one eavesdropping. He should be embarrassed, but he wasn't. She was unintentionally being his wingman.

She scrunched up her face. "You mean a date?"

Daria's tone sounded like she couldn't believe someone wanted to spend time with her. How could she think that? She was smart and beautiful and had a huge heart. "Of course. I have tickets to a ball game. The local team."

"The Revolution?" She lit up.

He couldn't help but smile back. "Yes, the Revolution."

"What time?"

Maybe he'd found something she might actually like. This romance was meant to be. "The game starts at five after seven. I could pick you up for dinner before, or we could eat there."

She cocked her head and studied him. "I'm not sure we should do that."

"Do what? Go on a date? I could play you owe me."

"Owe you?"

He gave her his best puppy dog eyes and leaned toward her. "I did spend a half hour with a Great Dane on my lap."

She laughed. "How long are you playing that card?"

Chapter Ten

The will stipulation was why he sat in the lobby of the Make Some Sunshine Foundation. Pictures of smiling children were plastered all over the royal blue walls. He couldn't remember ever being quite that happy as a child. Pauly had to sort out his inheritance and what charity was getting the money. He also realized if he didn't do some searching Jeeves would never approve of whatever charity he chose.

His neck itched from the tie, and he just wanted to get back to his car repair. The lobby was as sterile as an operating room. A fragrance he couldn't place permeated the windowed room. While he drummed his fingers on his leg, he bounced his other leg on the floor.

A polished woman, hair in a neat bun, strode over with an outstretched hand. Her heels clicked on the marble floor.

Each step was a countdown to Paul. She appeared ready to sell him on the charity.

"Mr. Vincenzo, nice to meet you. Come into my office."

A chill skittered down his spine from her thin, cold hands. Shouldn't the face for a charity be warmer?

She led the way down a short hallway to a sparsely furnished room. "Coffee?"

The desk was black lacquer and didn't have any drawers. A slim laptop sat on top, but no personal items in sight. He instantly disliked the woman. "I'm fine, thanks." He sat in a cheap, plastic chair. Why couldn't offices just have normal chairs?

"What brings you to our offices today?"

He shook himself, but the negative feelings about the place held onto him. He didn't like the vibe in here. "Dad's will states I have to give money to charity before I get my inheritance. I have to make sure the charity is real, worthwhile, and personal to me."

"I see." She forced her lips together. "Why us? Not that I'm not happy you're here." She said the last bit with a smile.

He liked that the office didn't come across as expensive. Probably meant not too many administrative costs. Most of the money went to the people the charity was supposed to help. That part was important. "I had to start somewhere, and kids getting last wishes seemed as good as any."

"Do you have kids?"

He shook his head. This charity was the fourth he'd interviewed. None of the rest of the charities impressed him, either. "No, I don't. I've never really been around them. I'm an only child though I have a million cousins." Paul was not sure why he told her that. None of those things mattered right now. As sweat trickled down his spine, he resisted the urge to rub his back in the chair. He had to rein things in or he'd be writing a meaningless check.

"Okay. We get about a thousand requests a month. We then review the requests in terms of feasibility; in other words, can we make this happen?" He rubbed a hand down his face. "The need of the child in terms of how sick is this child. Lastly, how much money do we have in the budget?"

"I see. Do you have a website or paperwork that talks about where the money goes?"

"I can assure you our administrative costs are low."

She figured out his angle. "I'd like to see that in print."

"Of course. I can get that paperwork. Uh, how much money are we talking about?"

He swallowed. He knew the answer but wasn't ready to reveal that.

****

Daria rested her elbows on the counter in her reception area, gazing at Shelley. "I shouldn't have agreed to go." The butterflies in Daria's stomach agreed. "What would Samuel think?"

Shelley rolled her eyes. "You're not dating him. You are just having a symbiotic relationship."

She'd had the same thought a day ago. "You make us sound like parasites."

Shelley laughed. She leaned back in her reception chair. "He gets you into society functions, and you are a nice accessory on his arm."

She shook her head. She remembered the shoe incident and how Samuel had frowned. "I'm not sure how I'm an accessory."

"You're a gorgeous woman. He wants one on his arm."

Daria waved away the suggestion. "That can't be the whole situation. He must have some affection for me."

"I'm sure he does, but he strikes me as pretty mercenary in his feelings."

"You make him out to be cold."

Shelley rested her chin on her hand. "Not cold, just calculating."

Daria wasn't sure her friend's assessment was correct. Though he'd never urged her for any further relationship than she wanted, Samuel had never seemed cold. Being with Samuel was comfortable.

"Speak of the devil." Shelley indicated the German car pulling into the first spot in the lot.

Samuel strode into the vet's office. "Daria, hello. Hello to you, too, Shelley." He smiled at both women.

Daria studied him. His smile wasn't cold or calculating. A preschooler could count how many times Samuel had come to her office. Then again, she'd only been to his work once. She didn't get to New York much. "What brings you here?"

He held a garment bag in one hand and a shoe box in the other. "I have something for you. For tonight?"

Daria searched her brain for what could possibly be happening this Saturday night. She couldn't remember. "Tonight?"

"I have another benefit. Cancer or heart disease or something," he said.

That event didn't sound familiar. "Did you tell me about this fundraiser? I'm sure I would have remembered."

Samuel cocked his head. "I didn't get a chance to tell you last night. Surely, you're free."

She didn't like the implication of Samuel's words. Daria's back stiffened. She wasn't at anyone's beck and call. Not any human, at least. "Well."

"She's not," Shelley piped in.

Samuel frowned. "I'm sure you can cancel your plans." He kept on talking. "Now I've brought a dress

85

and shoes. You'll look fantastic in them."

Daria didn't want to bail on her date with Paul. "I can't cancel."

While his brow knitted, Samuel shook his head.

Daria's stomach churned. The dread that coursed through her catapulted her back to when she gave Mom a report card that was not all A's. She was letting someone else down. "Well, maybe I could cancel."

Shelley glared. "No, you can't."

He stared through Shelley, who shrugged. "Daria, may we speak in private?"

Daria led Samuel to her office behind the reception desk. She sat in her chair.

He closed the door. "Daria, please. This event is important. And there will be a lot of people you can ask for money. This benefit will be good for both of us."

Daria sighed. He'd found a way to convince her. "Okay. I'll go." His broad smile didn't reach his eyes. She never noticed if the emotion ever did.

****

"Jeeves, I'm in trouble."

Because he'd needed Jeeves's help, Paul paced in the kitchen of the big house.

"What now, sir?" Jeeves asked.

He paused in his pacing. "I need tickets to tonight's Revolution game."

"You have a box that could be free tonight."

"I know I have a box. I don't want the box. I want to sit with everyone else."

Jeeves eyed him over his half-reading glasses. He was trying out a new recipe. A white apron was wrapped around his middle. Flour dotted his face. "With everyone else? What's with this need to slum lately?" Jeeves put a finger aside his nose.

If he'd had fifty pounds more on his frame, he'd have resembled Santa Claus.

"Could it be this woman?"

Rhetorical question. "Yes, it is. Can you help me?"

Jeeves nodded, then strolled to the phone on the wall.

The instrument reminded Paul of an old-fashioned wall phone but was truly modern.

Jeeves spoke quietly, then nodded, thanking the person.

After he hung up, he twisted to him. "There were still some available at the ballpark. You just have to pick them up at the will-call window."

"That was easy."

"Even you could have done that."

Paul laughed. "Are you saying I'm helpless?"

"In matters of the heart, yes. And in day-to-day things. You should get out from under your race cars more."

He had led a sheltered life, and he didn't know how to do simple things. He did know how to fix any car older than the year two thousand. "That reminds me. I have a car to fix before tonight."

****

Daria peeked in the mirror on the back of her office door and shook her head. The dress Samuel had brought made Daria look like a doll, but a less-endowed one. She hated the dress. How was she going to sit with ruffles by her butt? She spun one way, then the other.

Samuel smiled, shifting in the office chair.

He must approve, and his approval shouldn't matter.

"You'll look great."

As she looked back into the mirror at herself, Daria didn't agree. "I'm not sure I can wear this dress."

He frowned, staring at his phone. "Why not?"

The mirror wasn't full-length, but what she could see she wasn't happy with. She had cleavage for all to see. This wasn't her at all. With one last look in the mirror, she turned. "The bodice reveals way too much." The material was luxurious on her skin, but there wasn't enough.

Samuel shrugged. "That's the style. Besides, if you dazzle people, then they'll open their wallets to you."

She plopped into her chair. The dress rode up her legs, letting the world see most of her thighs. She tugged at the hem but to no avail. Because the ruffles were uncomfortable under her, she squirmed. "I feel like a loose woman."

"You're attending the event is for a good cause, isn't it?"

What about the animals she'd rescued last night? What about the animals she couldn't save? She stiffened her spine. Maybe this dress was for the best. Maybe she needed to trust Samuel. He hadn't steered her wrong yet. She let out a sigh. "I'll go. Dressed in something which makes me uncomfortable."

"You haven't put on the shoes."

She'd been dreading the shoes even more. The heels were higher than she'd ever worn. She would be in pain by the end of the night. Because she didn't sit very often, during the day she wore comfortable shoes. With a deep breath, she slipped them on and then stood. She wobbled. "Whoa."

Samuel caught her. "Steady. Take a few practice

steps."

She did, and her steps weren't any steadier. She pinwheeled her arms, but she caught herself on the edge of the desk. How was she getting from the car into the event? "I don't think I can walk in these."

"Just try."

She took a step, then a second. Her ankle gave out. She grabbed the desk and was thankful she didn't land on the floor. "These shoes aren't going to work."

"You'll get used to them."

"No, I won't."

Samuel frowned. "I really need you to do wear this dress and come with me."

She cocked her head, studying him. He'd never asked this much of her before tonight. His demands didn't make sense. He wanted her to dress differently all of a sudden. "Why? Why is this outfit important? You've brought me dresses before, but all were in my style."

"It just is. I better go. Practice." He waved and was out the door.

She couldn't chase him. "High heels are the Western equivalent of bound feet."

Shelley laughed from the doorway. "I can see cleavage."

Daria surveyed her outfit. Sure enough, her boobs were front and center. She didn't want to show her face outside the office dressed this way. She'd attract far too much attention. That wasn't her style. She was all about the animals. "Hmm. Can you sew?"

"A little."

"Let's see if we can alter this dress to my liking."

Chapter Eleven

Paul closed the hood of Daria's car, resting his hands on the metal and not liking what he'd seen. He didn't have good news. He'd have to take the head off the engine block. He didn't have her head gasket in stock, and ordering one might take a few days. As if the building had a better answer, he looked around his garage, but the building remained silent. As if in quiet observation, tools hung on the wall.

He wiped his hands with an already dirty rag, then checked his watch. Daria was at work, and maybe that wasn't the best place to give bad news, but the sooner he had clearance to order the part the better. Having programmed her office number into his cell, he only needed one hand to dial. He leaned on the hood, waiting for the call to go through.

Shelley answered.

"This is Paul. Can I talk to Daria?"

"Sure thing."

A male voice told him his call was important and continued to list their hours and the services they provided. He preferred classical music.

"Paul," Daria answered on the phone.

She sounded more serious than usual. Now he was worried. Had something happened to the dog? "Is something wrong?"

"Spike's fine. He kept all of his food down today.

He's in better spirits."

"That's great." He paused, not sure he could sugarcoat his bad news. "Your car isn't so good. I'll need to take the engine apart."

"Oh? How long will that take?"

He surveyed his garage to see what other projects he had on his plate. The part wouldn't come for a day. He gave her his best estimate. "A day or two. I can probably loan you a car in the meantime."

She paused. "No, that's okay."

The silence sounded full. Something else was going on, and he had a sneaking suspicion he wasn't going to be happy. He couldn't catch a break.

"Something's come up, and I have to break our date."

Was she seeing someone else like that stuffy guy at the benefit? He longed to ask that question. If she was involved with someone, that was none of his business. He didn't know her well enough. He rubbed a hand down his face, the oil on his hand making it glide. "Okay. We can go another time. Is everything okay?"

"Yes, things are fine. You can pick up Spike on Monday. We're closed tomorrow, and I'd like to keep him here another day."

Was he taking Spike? "Whatever you think."

"Thanks for being understanding. I'm sure you are eager to get your dog back."

Not really. He hadn't decided to keep the dog. Maybe Daria could find him a new home. Now was not the time to broach that subject. He leaned against the wall. "May I call you tomorrow?"

"I'll check on Spike in the morning, if you want to wait until then to call me. Or I can call you."

"Either way. Have a good evening, Daria."

"Good night, Paul."

Now he had tickets for a baseball game he had no desire to attend alone. Even the silence on his phone sounded lonely.

****

As if he enjoyed saying it, her name on Paul's tongue sounded warm to Daria. As she sat in her office chair, that warmth wrapped around her like a blanket. She replaced the receiver sorry she wasn't spending the evening with him. A baseball game in jeans and a T-shirt was preferable to what she was actually doing.

Now she had just half an hour to fix her hair and learn to move better on these shoes. She slipped the shoes back on and stomped around, turning off lights. Practical was her middle name.

Shelley was home, eating dinner probably.

That left this task as Daria's responsibility. She sighed. Domestic life sounded charming, but she wasn't sure if she was cut out for that life. No man had ever been patient with her focus on the animals. With one last "Goodnight" to the dogs, she hobbled over to her cottage behind her office. "Thirty minutes to beautiful hair."

She harrumphed and set about making herself presentable, despite her not being into going out tonight. Her curly locks were not to be tamed, but she did her best. Samuel would appreciate her effort.

When he picked her up thirty minutes later on the dot, he did.

"Wow." He helped her into his car, closing the door.

"I hope whatever you are trying to prove works.

And is worth your time," she said. *This car was too much.*

****

"She's here," someone squealed.

Daria recognized the voice. She remembered the nasal quality from only hearing Carmela days ago. Maria and Carmela were here at the benefit. This fundraiser was another ballroom in another event space where people dressed up and paid money to eat food they could make at home. She shouldn't be cynical, but she was uncomfortable in these clothes.

As he looked over her shoulder, Samuel grimaced.

Daria could imagine how he viewed them, but she refused to let him disparage her relatives. "Be nice." She swung around to smile.

Carmela and Maria embraced her like they were high school chums.

Daria didn't know how to respond, so she patted each of their backs. The motion was the best she could do. When they let go of her, she stumbled.

Samuel snagged her arm

She flashed him a grateful smile. "Carmela, Maria, this is Samuel."

He shook each woman's hand. "Charmed." Then he glanced at Daria for explanations.

She hadn't told him about Mario.

She pinched him. "These are my sisters, Samuel."

He switched on his thousand-watt smile, the one he saved for clients. "Really nice to meet Daria's family."

Carmela studied Samuel up and down. "You her boyfriend?"

The word catapulted out of his mouth. "No." He shrugged.

He wasn't wrong, but why was he quick to disavow any relationship? Something was up with him tonight. Daria shook her head. "No, Samuel and I are friends." Daria studied the two women and suddenly realized they'd been the ones staring at the last benefit. The one where she'd met Paul. Now she understood.

"Friends," Carmela echoed. "Do you have seats?"

Samuel tugged her arm. "Yes, we do. We'll need to find them. Nice meeting you, Carmela, Maria."

With that, Samuel whisked her away.

Daria waved at her sisters, wishing she could have talked to them longer.

****

Fresh from the shower, Paul wandered into the kitchen in the big house.

Jeeves sat at the island, eating his dinner and reading the paper.

He studied him for a moment. He often wondered what his real name was. Jeeves was raised on the streets of Newark. His British accent was an affectation which he had done for so long he didn't know how to talk any other way. For a kid from the streets, he'd done well. Maybe someday, Jeeves would tell him. "Hey, Jeeves."

Jeeves lifted his gaze. "Pauly. There's some dinner in the oven, if you are interested."

Once again, Jeeves to the rescue. When he entered the room, garlic assaulted him. "I've been stood up. How did you know?"

Jeeves shook his head. "I didn't. I always make extra."

He patted him on the back. "You're a good man, Jeeves, but I have a mind to go out."

"You still have the invitation to the Cancer Society

94

Benefit. Attending might help you choose where the money will go."

Paul stifled a groan. Another night in a monkey suit was not his idea of a good time. Still, he had to figure out a charity he liked. Maybe Daria's animals would do. "I'm working on donating that money."

"You do have a deadline which is fast approaching."

The clock was ticking, and if he didn't find a worthy charity, he'd lose everything including the house, his business, and Vinny's Weenies. He would even lose Jeeves. He sighed. Maybe the charity event was necessary tonight. "Is my tux home from the cleaners?"

Jeeves waved a hand. "In your closet, in your old bedroom upstairs."

"Maybe I'll go then."

"Dateless? How unlike you, Pauly."

He'd never gone out dateless. He found the idea interesting. He could leave the event when he wanted. The hour was too late to call Carmela. "Why not? Set the tongues wagging." Paul left the room. Jeeves was already back to his reading.

As promised, his tux was waiting, and the fit was perfect. He'd stopped going to benefits with Dad long ago. He'd found them stuffy and full of the same people having the same conversations. He'd only started again when the stipulation of the will had been revealed.

Checking himself in the mirror one more time, he vowed to have a good time, no matter what.

Chapter Twelve

As soon as she arrived at their table at the benefit, Daria understood why Samuel wanted to parade her around the place. His ex-girlfriend was there with her new fiancée. She sported a rock even Samuel couldn't have afforded. His obvious pain was the only thing which made her forget his rude behavior toward Carmela and Maria.

She wanted to run screaming from the event taking place at a grand hotel so far out of her budget she wouldn't see if she squinted. She didn't care that her looks paled in comparison to most women here. That fact didn't bother her. Samuel's treachery was an issue. She should have suspected something. "This act is pretty low of you, Samuel." Daria spoke under her breath

"I had no idea she'd be here."

"Right. I need to powder my nose." She spun away. She needed time to think and plan her way home. She wasn't spending the evening with Samuel eyeing his ex.

He held her. "There is plenty of powder on that nose."

She tugged, her arm finally coming free. She stumbled on the stilettos and then recovered. "I'll be back. At least, get me some champagne." Wending her way through the crowd, she found the ladies' room and plopped herself on a stool. She stared, not liking how she looked, even after Shelley had sewn the bodice to it was less revealing. This dress wasn't her style, nor was this dress how she wanted to present herself to the world. She was a veterinarian, for goodness' sake, not a model. "I look like a tart."

Think of the animals. Spike entered her mind, and even though he wasn't one she saved, he could be a poster dog for the ones who had yet to be saved. Maybe she was viewing this situation all wrong. This night could be a chance to play a role or step out of her comfort zone. She didn't think she could accomplish that, but she had to try. Fixing her lipstick, she vowed to hold her head high. "He wants a trophy on his arm? He'll get one." But she would still further her agenda. "Remember the animals." She strode out of the ladies' room.

Samuel stood at the bottom of a flight of steps into the ballroom. He held two glasses of champagne.

One of which she assumed was hers. She took the first step with care, holding onto the railing. On the second step, she placed her foot with more assurance. The third step did her in. She twisted an ankle and, in a dance akin to a marionette, she flailed one arm while she hung onto the railing. She steadied herself, taking in the room.

No one had seen her. Or so she assumed. After a deep breath, she took the last step, only shifting her weight to the lower foot when she was confident the limb would hold her.

Someone had spilled a few drops of their drink, making the floor an ice rink.

Daria had no idea how to skate, and she lost her

footing.

Strong arms caught her.

She would have smacked her head on the steps otherwise.

"You okay?" a deep and familiar voice asked.

She connected visually with Paul Vincenzo. She saw amusement and concern in his eyes. "Paul."

He righted her but didn't let go. "So, this event was what you blew me off for."

His voice held no rancor. Should she explain? "I need cash for my shelter. At one of these, I can get more money than any direct mail campaign."

He glanced around the large room. "These people have deep pockets."

Samuel strode over. "Daria?"

Daria waved a hand between them. "Paul Vincenzo. Samuel Lafayette."

The two men shook hands, sizing each other up.

Samuel spoke first. "Why do you have your hands on my date?"

He didn't let go. "Because she almost fell. I never understand why women wear shoes this high."

Samuel took her arm. "Because they look good in them. Daria, I have a few people for you to meet."

"Make sure she doesn't fall," Paul called after them.

"Could we not talk about me as if I weren't here?" Daria wrested her arm from Samuel and limped off in the direction he had come from.

"You're hurt," Samuel said.

Paul reached her first.

"I'm fine," Daria said.

He touched her leg. "No, look, your ankle is

swelling."

This situation couldn't get more embarrassing. So much for channeling an inner trophy wife. She wasn't succeeding at all. "I'll walk off the pain."

Paul shook his head, his brow knit. "I'm not sure that's a good idea."

Samuel caught her arm and directed her away. "She's fine. She has people to meet."

Daria limped along with Samuel, but not before she shot a frown back. She didn't want to be manhandled by anyone, so she once again retrieved her arm from Samuel's grip.

Paul glanced away.

Carmela appeared at his side.

He hugged her.

Daria wondered how they knew each other. But her date was way ahead, so she couldn't stop to ask. "Slow down, Samuel."

He did but frowned.

When he faced her nowadays, that was always his expression. His displeasure poured from his frown lines. She couldn't please him and wondered why she bothered. She hobbled along behind him, in case he was actually going to introduce her to someone.

He finally stopped and put a hand on her back to guide her towards two people. "Daria, meet Mr. and Mrs. Gaudette."

The auburn-haired woman stood just inches shorter than her husband. He sported a dark, neatly-trimmed beard which made his steely eyes even sharper. "Nice to meet you," Daria said.

"Call me Jennifer."

"I'm Daria."

Her husband introduced himself as Sean, but he didn't linger on her. Instead, he looked back at his wife as if she were the only woman in the room.

No one had ever looked at Daria that way. She sighed. She didn't think anyone ever would. Shaking herself, she launched into her sales pitch for the shelter.

Sean and Jennifer nodded. Then they wrote a check.

She marveled at the idea they carried their checkbook with them in this day and age. She'd expected them to send her money. She wasn't going to complain because she had a real-life check in her hand. With an amount large enough to renovate her building, Daria had a purpose. Her ankle pain couldn't impinge on her happiness.

Samuel directed her to their table.

Paul already sat there, speaking to someone. He smiled, but his attention rolled back to the other woman.

Daria never considered herself a jealous person, but that emotion was what she was feeling. She sat, but she knocked one of the forks off the table.

Samuel picked up the utensil but showed no expression. Samuel kissed her cheek. "I'll be right back, dear."

Did he kiss her for Paul's benefit? Since she'd gone to the bathroom, Samuel had chosen another table. She guessed the first one had filled in her absence. Samuel had never been particularly affectionate. They weren't a real couple. Theirs was a business arrangement.

He wended his way to the table where his ex-girlfriend sat.

She smiled at his back. He was such a man, always pining for the one that got away.

"How's your ankle?"

Paul's voice made her jump. "Fine, I guess."

He didn't move away. "You get money from that couple?"

She smiled. "Yes, I did." No date was in sight.

He sat. He tugged at Daria's leg. "Let me see."

Shifting, she lifted her foot onto his lap. She winced.

He slid off her right shoe. "Look at that. I could barely remove this shoe."

Daria waved a hand. "I'll be fine."

He frowned at her shoe, turning them over in his hand. "Why do you wear these things?"

She shrugged. "They were Samuel's idea."

Paul glanced at Samuel, then back to her. He lifted his eyebrows. "He looks to be making time with another woman."

She glanced in the direction he indicated.

Samuel laughed and smiled at everything the woman said.

"She is his ex-girlfriend. She's engaged."

Paul gazed at her. "So no threat?"

Since she wasn't involved with Samuel, no one was a threat. "She isn't a threat." Even though he'd asked her on a date, she wasn't explaining herself. The now-evident foot pain was making her petulant. His warm hands roved over her right foot, which was swollen. She winced. She wouldn't get the shoe back on. She'd stroll out of here, wearing no shoes like a bridesmaid who had too much to drink.

He patted her uninjured leg. "Let me take you

home."

She stared deep into his concerned eyes, without any anger. His reaction touched her soul. "I came with Samuel."

He looked over her left shoulder. "He doesn't look ready to leave."

She looked at Paul. Neither of them had eaten. "You don't either."

He shrugged. "Daria, your foot is swollen. I'm sure you've had enough campaigning for animals for one night."

She was tired and getting irritable. He was right. That fact didn't make her happy. The check she'd received should be enough, and the way her mood was going she wasn't making any new friends. "I should at least tell Samuel I'm leaving."

Paul looked in Samuel's direction. "He might not miss you."

She raised an eyebrow at the statement.

He patted a calf. "Not that you aren't miss-able, he just is too busy with his tongue hanging out over there."

She couldn't argue that point. The whole room had receded in Samuel's mind. Gloria, his ex, could walk on water. If they were a real couple, then Daria might be jealous. "At least, let me leave him a note."

"Suit yourself." He pulled out a gold pen from a pocket. A business card appeared also. "Here."

She admired the pen and wondered if a customer left the item. Mechanics didn't usually carry things this expensive. "Thanks. What about your date?"

"I didn't come with one."

She wrote and then left the card at Samuel's place. "May I have my shoe?"

Paul shook his head. "You are not walking out of here in those."

She was ready for a fight.

Chapter Thirteen

The outside air had turned cooler and had a hint of rain. Daria managed the few steps outside the hotel but doubted she could go any farther. She held onto Paul who didn't seem to mind.

The valet pulled up with an expensive car.

Daria glanced at Paul. He showed no expression. This vehicle wasn't the wrong car. This car was more expensive than Samuel's.

He shrugged. "I borrowed the car."

She shook her head. "I didn't think that was yours. Mechanics don't make that much." She bit her tongue. That statement was rude.

The valet opened the door to the classy car.

This one she'd never seen before now. Her grip loosened, and she grimaced when she put weight on her bad ankle.

Wrong.

She shifted off her bad foot, but that appendage decided not to support her.

His grip tightened.

Too bad her pin-wheeling loosened his hold. She ended up knocking his hands off of her. The resulting landing on her bottom was inevitable. Did she go down gracefully? Like a lady? Of course not. She fell butt over teakettle with legs flying and arms flailing. She was a viral video waiting to happen. Or had happened, but no one was around to see. She thanked the universe for small favors.

The momentum only stopped after her butt hit the pavement. Her downfall splashed water on the valet's shoes. That moisture was soaking into her dress.

The valet and Paul rushed to help her. "Daria, I'm so sorry."

"That one was all mine."

Back into the land of the upright, she sighed.

A frown creased his face. "Are you sure you're okay?"

She nodded, a smile dancing across her lips. "Nothing wounded but my pride."

"Come, get in the car, Daria."

When she was safely in seated at her lowest potential energy state, she glanced back.

Lines crossed his brow.

She smiled.

"You don't think I can afford this car?" he asked.

His tone held no accusation, but he closed the door before she could answer. As usual, she'd put her foot in her mouth. Shelley often said to think before she spoke. She didn't know how.

He slid onto the driver's seat. He chewed on the side of his mouth, a myriad of emotions crossing his face. "I lied. This car is mine."

Daria studied the leather seat. "You don't have to impress me. I like you already."

He chuckled. "I'm glad to hear that. Now, let's get you home and get some ice on that ankle."

She had to ask. "Why were you at the benefit?"

"Did you get some money from that couple?"

She let him distract her. She settled into the butter

leather seat that cupped her as if she were fine china. "Yes."

The drive didn't take long. Paul pulled into the parking lot of the vet office and drove around the back the way she directed him.

"Sit. I'll come around."

She didn't like to be coddled. She'd spent a lot of life taking care of herself. "I'm okay."

He put a warm hand on an arm. "Let me take care of you."

Her spine stiffened. "I can take care of myself."

"I'm sure you can, but right now, you can't walk."

He slid out of the car before she could argue. She opened the door, took one step out, then fell into his arms. "Whoa."

He swept her up into his grasp. "I'll take things from here." With his face inches away, he stared at her lips, and he cleared his throat. "You have your key?"

She pulled out a dog key chain from the clutch she held. "Right here." Unlocking the door, she insisted he didn't have to come in. "I can walk."

He shook his head.

She searched her memory for the last time she ran a vacuum.

"No, I will deliver you to your couch." He did as he promised. "Let me get some ice for that foot. Which way is the kitchen?

After pointing him in the right direction, she settled against the cushions, uncomfortable at being waited on enveloping her. Time to make a joke. "I think maybe I could get used to this level of pampering."

"Yeah?" He spoke from the kitchen. "You waiting for a prince to sweep you off of your feet?"

She laughed. "No, I just want someone with a big wallet, so I can save more animals."

When he returned, he cocked his head.

"Just kidding, Paul."

He put a dishtowel and then a bag of ice on her right ankle.

He was gentle. She still winced at the cold.

"Everything you do is about the animals, isn't it?"

Daria studied his face. "Is there something wrong with that?"

He settled on the coffee table. "Sometimes, people do that to the detriment of humans."

"I don't think animals are better than humans. Let me rephrase. Unlike humans, animals are never intentionally vicious. They only know how to be nice. Unless someone mistreats them."

"Spoken like a woman who has encountered vicious people."

She thought of Mario and the brutal life Mom had protected her from by not acknowledging him. Now, he was doing his best to take care of her. How could a man raised in such an environment have such a big heart? As a child, she'd hated him. Now, as an adult, she understood just what he kept her from experiencing. She never stopped being grateful for no one knowing who her father was. "Not vicious, but no humans can give unconditional love. There is always a catch."

"That's awfully cynical."

A shrug rippled through her shoulders. "Maybe, but not untrue."

He frowned. "I don't agree. A parent is supposed to give his child unconditional love."

"But they don't always."

He never looked away. Granted she was the just other person in the room, but he hadn't even really studied the place. She found his gaze unnerving.

For a moment, he stared over her left shoulder.

She wondered if he had encountered an example of conditional love. "Maybe not." Daria didn't often have anyone over to her little cottage and certainly no dates. Having Paul here was comfortable. "So, how does a mechanic afford such an expensive car?"

He laughed. "You're changing the subject."

She leaned back into the pillows. "Yes. This conversation is too deep for a Saturday night."

He leaned forward, resting his forearms on his thighs. "You hungry?"

"Starving."

He cocked his head toward the kitchen. "Mind if I poke around in your refrigerator?"

Frowning, she waved a hand over her right shoulder. "I have some frozen vegetarian dinners."

He shook his head. "I need meat."

"You won't find meat here."

His face screwed up for a moment. "Are you a vegan?"

Daria shook her head. "No, I'm not that strict."

He nodded. "Then I'll make us some omelets."

Delight rolled through her. "You cook?"

****

As he cooked, Paul hummed. He couldn't imagine being anywhere else. He undid the bow tie, then removed his jacket, and slid them both onto a chair. The tiny kitchen had all the appliances, but not a lot of counter space. The room was cute just like Daria.

The refrigerator was harvest gold and had the

freezer on top, but if the appliance worked, why get rid of it? The linoleum under his feet was a little soft.

She was a practical woman.

He found a pan and rummaged through the cabinet for herbs. With the pan heating, he beat the eggs with a practiced skill. He loved making breakfast. The rest of the day's meals weren't so easy.

"Something smells great."

He smiled. While he delivered Daria a glass of white wine, he left the omelet set.

She thanked him and took a sip. She wrinkled her nose.

He didn't think he said anything wrong. "What?"

She shook her head. "Sneeze." She sucked in a few breaths, waving a hand in front of her nose and widening her eyes

He didn't understand.

So, she would sneeze.

He did all the time.

Just when she was about to sneeze, Paul realized the problem. He grabbed the glass out of her left hand.

The sneeze shook her whole body. She sniffed afterward. "Thanks. I would have been wearing my wine."

"Welcome." He handed her a tissue and her glass. "Food will be done in a minute." He strolled to the kitchen and then back with two placemats and two sets of silverware.

"You're pretty domestic."

He shrugged. "Mom made sure I knew the basics of cooking."

"Good woman."

"In her own way, yes." He smiled before returning

for the food. "Your meal, madame." With a flourish, he put the plates down.

She widened her eyes, and she gazed back to him. "You even garnished them."

"We aim to please."

She took a bite and closed her eyes.

He didn't know why her opinion was important, but he held his breath until she finished. He wanted her to love what he cooked.

"Wow. Eggs don't taste this way when I cook them. What did you put in them?"

He settled on a wicker chair opposite her. He took a bite. The fluffy eggs danced across his palette. "Nothing special."

"These eggs are so light and fluffy."

He shrugged. "Just takes arm strength to whip them correctly."

She nodded, then shifted so her feet were planted on the floor. The bag of ice hit the carpeting. "That's probably true." She picked up the plastic bag and put it on the table. "You're a man of many talents."

The idea she liked him, sent warmth through him. He shrugged. "I get by."

She took a few more bites. "Where did you learn to fix cars?"

He finished chewing. "Shop class in high school." He'd been interested long before high school. A neighbor had a pony car, and he'd been entranced by the vehicle. The man taught a very young Paul some basics, and he was hooked. Then Dad had bought one, too.

"Of course."

"Well, the choice was either to learn to fix things

properly or drive my parents nuts taking their appliances apart."

She giggled. "I took in all of the stray animals in the neighborhood."

Not surprised by her revelations, he nodded. Something early in both of their lives still affected them. "Fixed broken bird wings and all that."

"Yes. Mom convinced one of her boyfriends to build a shed, so I wouldn't bring the 'filthy things' as she called them, into the house."

"She didn't see your interest as a viable career?"

She shook her head. What little hair was not piled on top swirled around. "No, she just assumed that my actions were part of a phase, and I'd come to my senses."

He eyed her. "Which meant?"

She wrinkled her nose. "That I'd marry a doctor."

"Oh. Guess she's disappointed."

She looked past him. "Yes, she was. She passed a few years ago."

"Sorry for your loss."

She shook herself. "Thanks for making this meal and for coming to my rescue. Seems I owe you for a bunch of things."

"Then let me take you out tomorrow. Ice skating."

She glanced at her right ankle, frowning.

He laughed. What was he thinking? "Okay, not ice skating. What would you like to do?"

"The dogs need some exercise. We could take them to that new dog park?"

"Dog park?"

"Just south of here on this road. You can let them run free, and they get to socialize with other dogs."

Dog park. He'd never been to a dog park, but if he was there with Daria, he'd probably enjoy himself. Whatever she wanted to do was fine with him. He just wanted to spend time and get to know her better. "Is that good?"

"Yes, it is. You can find out how Spike is with other dogs."

"I don't really know."

"You wouldn't."

How could he let her down? He should keep Spike. She might think worse of him if he didn't. When had he cared what other people thought? Maybe he only cared what Daria thought of him. "No, not really. I just…"

Chapter Fourteen

Daria grabbed the phone off the side table, punching the button to answer with more force than she probably should have. "Daria, here." She should have looked at the number, but the list of people who called was short. She settled back into the couch.

"It's Samuel. I wanted to make sure you were okay."

Guess he finally noticed she was gone. Movement made the pain in her ankle increased. "I am now. I twisted my ankle on these awful shoes. I'm not wearing them again. Maybe you can return them."

"I can come by tomorrow and pick them up," Samuel said.

She looked around at Paul. "I'm not sure when I'm going to be here."

He had finished and cleaned their dinner plates.

She could hear him in the kitchen, running water into the sink. He didn't have to do the dishes. She appreciated that he was willing to do them.

"Oh? You have plans?" Samuel asked.

Samuel was getting on her last nerve. How dare he think she had nothing better to do than wait! Friends shouldn't treat each other in that manner. "I have a life away from you, Samuel."

"I know that, but do you have a life away from those dogs?"

She chuckled. "I'm taking them for a walk."

"Oh. Count me out."

Relief washed over her. Paul was in her home. She couldn't have Samuel here. Neither of them had a claim on her. She shrugged. "Paul Vincenzo drove me home."

"Wasn't that nice of him?"

A touch of venom tinged his voice. She couldn't imagine Samuel was jealous.

"I have another benefit on Friday night."

She glanced back into the kitchen. "As long as I can dress in my own clothes, I'll go."

He chuckled. "I learned my lesson, Daria. Besides, I might actually be over Gloria."

Finally. She'd been hearing about the ex since they broke up. The breakup had prompted Samuel to ask her to come to benefits with him. She rested her head on the soft cushion of the back of the couch. "You've been apart for a year."

"But we dated for a long time."

Was she being too harsh? "I know, Samuel, you have to grieve however long you need."

"That was awfully trite."

She laughed. "I guess my words were." She yawned. "I'm going now. I'll call you tomorrow about those shoes." She disconnected.

Paul was still in the kitchen.

She limped into the room. Her ankle didn't hurt as much anymore. She might be okay to work tomorrow.

He pulled out a chair. "Sit."

"I'm okay. My ankle doesn't hurt."

"You'll be okay to walk tomorrow?"

She nodded. The swelling had gone down. "I'm sure. No permanent damage."

He smiled. "Good. Let me get out of your hair."

"You want to take Spike home?"

He hesitated. "Tonight?"

"Yes, I'll give you some dog food to try. If he still gets sick, we can try something else."

Would Spike respond?

****

What was he doing with a dog? Paul's pulse raced. He didn't have anything to care for an animal. He didn't even know what he would need. Praying for an all-night grocery store, he loaded Spike into his car behind Happy Valley Veterinary. This dog made him tired. The night had cooled further, and he was thankful he wore a jacket.

"This car isn't ideal for transporting a dog," Daria mentioned. She'd slipped into sneakers, but she still wore her dress and stockings. Somehow, the outfit was charming.

The lone light outside the house cast a yellow glow.

She didn't limp as much. He was sure she'd be fine in the morning. Of course, he'd be here to be certain. "I think Spike and I will do fine." He smiled.

She smiled back.

He leaned in and kissed her cheek. He wanted to do more, but he chose to take his time with Daria. She deserved the best and deserved for him to woo her. "This evening was fun. I don't often get to cook for anyone."

"I don't often get cooked for."

That fact was sad. Daria deserved to be pampered and taken care of the way she took care of animals. He could be the man who could do that pampering. He wanted to be the man to do that taking care of her. "We'll have to see about changing that." He slid into the driver's seat and then started the car. "Tomorrow."

She waved.

Spike licked the window.

Paul rolled down the window an inch. That action made the dog happy.

The critter sniffed at the incoming air, and his tongue stuck out the side of his snout.

He stopped at a supermarket for a leash and bowls and a toy or two. At the last moment, he put some rawhide chews into the basket.

The neon lights of the supermarket made this all feel apocalyptic.

The young woman at the checkout smiled. "Just get a dog?"

"He's visiting." Paul still wasn't sure if he was keeping the dog. He didn't know if he could actually handle the responsibility. He'd never had to take care of anything or anyone other than himself. On their trip tomorrow, he'd tell Daria the truth.

Spike stared at him on the way back.

The dog was melting his heart. He didn't know if he could be a good dog owner. Maybe Spike would be better with someone else. He glanced around the interior of the car. "You didn't chew anything, that's good. Let's keep the car clean, okay?"

Spike licked his face.

He took that response as an answer. "Boy, I hope you're housebroken."

****

Paul drove past to get to his apartment, and the lights were off at the big house. Jeeves was in bed.

Tires crunched over gravel as he parked his car beside the garage. His car already smelled like dog.

The one-bedroom apartment seemed empty now that he'd been at Daria's. He looked around and realized he hadn't put much of his personality into the place. He put together some blankets for the dog to sleep on. He placed them next to his bed in the tiny apartment above his garage.

The dog lay on the bed.

He exited the bathroom. He didn't know why, but he made room and didn't chase off the dog. The sheets would smell like a dog. He sneezed. Was he coming down with a cold? "You being cute is a good thing."

He wasn't sorry until early the next day after the dog licked his face and whined. He catapulted out of bed, not realizing what or who was licking him. He put a hand over his racing heart. "You. Don't you sleep in?"

Spike whined.

"You have to go out?" He sneezed. After shoving feet into shoes, he pulled a shirt over his head. "Be right with you." He sneezed again. "I must be coming down with a cold." He searched for the leash, then decided the dog didn't need to be tethered.

Spike ran out the open door.

Paul couldn't stop him. "Come back, Spike."

The dog raced in the direction of the big house, stopping to wet some trees along the way.

The air was cool, but no rain had fallen all night. Not dressed for chasing a dog, he ran after him anyway. He stopped, out of breath, and then continued. He found the dog sitting quietly, staring at Jeeves.

"Is this animal a dog?" Jeeves asked.

"What do you think?"

Jeeves looked at him over half-glasses. "I think you're in over your head with this woman if she has you taking on a dog."

Paul was too out of breath to laugh. Maybe he was in over his head. How could he start a relationship until his inheritance was settled? Bad timing, but he liked Daria a lot. He didn't want to wait or give her up. "How'd you stop him?"

Jeeves shrugged. "I come from a long line of butlers. I have ancestors who were butlers to royalty, and we took care of the dogs, too."

He couldn't help but laugh. "Jeeves, you grew up in the ironbound section of Newark. Your ancestors are Portuguese."

Jeeves rose to his full height. "Then we butlered for royalty in Portugal. Either way, the dog listened to me."

"Why?"

A smile creased Jeeves thin face. "Because he thinks I'm the leader of the pack."

Paul ran a hand through his hair. "Yeah? Then you can take care of him while I take a shower." He turned back toward the apartment, relieved the dog was in good hands for the moment. What was he going to do long term? Obedience classes?

"Has he been fed?" Jeeves asked.

"Nope, I have his stuff down here."

"Bring his things when you finish."

Could he get Jeeves to train his dog, too?

Chapter Fifteen

Daria walked around her house the next morning, but she had no pain. In fact, her step was lighter. The prospect of spending some time with Paul elated her. She headed out for breakfast, a rare treat, instead of the usual cereal. The diner down the road was within walking distance, and she hummed her whole trip home.

The sun was in its full glory, warming her.

When she saw a sign for Vinny's Weenies sat on the property she'd wanted to buy, she paused. "Of all things next to my office. I'll have to smell hot dogs all day." She shrugged off her discomfort. She wouldn't let this turn of events ruin the day. The diner was busy, so she sat at the counter.

The same server who had waited on her and Paul approached. "What can I get you?"

Daria gave her an order of yogurt with berries. She could have eaten that dish at home, but today would be different and maybe a new beginning. She planned to spend the morning with a man. Not just any man, but one interested and who stared as if she were the only woman in the room. She didn't know what the future held, but today, the future appeared bright.

He was waiting with Spike. He was talking.

As if he understood every single word, Spike stared. The dog's expression reminded her of something from a Hallmark card.

While the man smiled, Spike barked.

She bent to pet Spike.

He licked her face.

The feel of dog saliva never got old. "You been waiting long?"

Paul shook his head, a smile on his face. "No. We just pulled in."

She looked down at Spike. "How's he doing?"

"Okay, but he doesn't listen. He ran away this morning."

She cocked her head. "You don't know how to be a pack leader."

"No." He paused. "I have a confession."

Just then, Spike threw up on the driveway.

Daria jumped out of the way, so just a little splattered on her. She wiped off a shoe in a patch of grass. Then she realized Paul might be grossed out. She looked at him. He seemed more concerned about the dog. "Did you feed him the food I gave you?"

"Uh, yes, but I think my bu—my friend might have given him something else, too."

She shook her head. "He shouldn't have people's food. At all. Not a scrap. His stomach is too sensitive."

"I'll remember to tell my friend that, Daria."

"He seems okay, now. His spirits are good. Maybe he's fine." She stood and then brushed off where he'd left dirty paw prints. "You had something to say? Walk with me, while I get one or two of the other dogs." She glanced back at his car. "Can we take your car since mine is in your shop?"

He smiled. "Guess we have no choice."

"Thanks." She strode toward the back of her office

and then unlocked a door.

Paul followed.

She stopped short. She took two leashes off hooks, then opened one cage to connect one to a rescued dog's collar. She did the same for the other. "Would you like some pointers on care?"

He sighed. "I wasn't sure I'm keeping Spike."

She put a hand on her fluttering heart. Why? "Not keeping him? I'm sure we can work through any problem behaviors. I'd hate to see him back in a shelter. The more times he goes back to the shelter, the harder to find him a home."

"Oh." He blinked.

He obviously didn't like that idea any more than she did. She had worked with some hard-to-place dogs, and they'd ended up fine. Spike wasn't difficult at all. She smiled. "Let's load them up. The dog park isn't far."

****

The dog park was empty except for the dogs Paul and Daria had brought. The space consisted of trees and fire hydrants with benches for the owners to sit on.

A gentle breeze moved the leaves on the trees. Paul zipped up his jacket.

She let them loose.

He mulled over what to say. He wanted Daria to like him, but he wasn't pretending to be something he wasn't. *What will she think of me if I give back this dog?* Technically, the dog wasn't even his.

She didn't care. She was sure he could take care of the animal.

He wasn't. She'd be disappointed. He didn't want to be the one to do what to Daria.

The dogs frolicked like old friends in the fence-enclosed area.

He was surprised at the lack of dog poop. The place didn't smell.

"You're quiet." She threw a ball.

Spike jumped in the air to catch it.

"Wow. He'd be good for agility training," she said. "The training would take the edge off of his energy, and he'd behave better."

He did have room on the property. Could he assign the task to Jeeves to get the training done? Paul had a lot in his brain, and he couldn't imagine taking on another task.

The day had dawned sunny with a light breeze. Fluffy white clouds drifted over them. The day couldn't have been more perfect. He refocused on what Daria had said. "Agility training?"

"They jump through hoops and over things. The dogs have fun. Gives them a job." She stood close.

Close enough to smell vanilla. He resisted the urge to lean in and sniff her. He'd leave that action to Spike, but the vanilla scent filled his nostrils. He didn't even know if he wanted the dog. She had him training him.

What was she thinking?

What was he thinking? "I can't even get him to sit for me."

"Really?" Her attention slid back to the dogs. "Come, Spike."

The black dog trotted over, tail wagging enough to smack himself on each side.

He'd never seen a dog this happy.

"Sit."

The dog did as she said. Of course, she possessed

the knack. She dealt with dogs all day.

Daria shrugged. "You try." She released the dog from his sitting position.

Paul gave the command a try. "Sit, Spike."

The dog stared at him.

Daria laughed. "I'm sorry. He just doesn't see you as above him in his pack."

He frowned. "That's the second time I've heard that today."

"Yeah?"

Paul waved his hands. "Jeeves got him to sit."

"Jeeves?"

"A friend."

"Sounds like a butler's name."

He laughed. She had no idea how close she was to the truth. "So, how do I get him to recognize my dominance?"

"Just work with him. Maybe alone. Keep him on the leash until he obeys you."

Great, just what he had time for. The dog viewed him, possibly gauging his reaction. Paul shrugged off the idea. The dog couldn't understand what they were saying. "I'll try when we get home."

"I'm sure once you settle that, he'll be a great dog. You can try obedience classes, too. Shelley offers some once a week. I'll ask her if there's an opening."

His world tilted on its axis. All he did was bring the dog to the vet, and now he was in obedience classes with this dog. Boy, what he'd do for a woman.

****

Back at the office, Daria put the dogs in their cages after an hour at the park. Since Paul had asked her out to lunch, she found a place for Spike.

The rest of the dogs barked for attention, and he flinched.

The noise level could get high in that room when the cages were full. She was used to the noise. The air had piqued her hunger, causing her stomach to rumble.

"Guess we're eating just in time." He stood close.

Since their discussion about Spike, he'd been quiet. She hoped she hadn't overstepped in giving him advice. They'd met just two days ago. She didn't know much about him. She could take this lunch to find out. Because she would have a meal with Paul, her mood from earlier was still in place and even rose. She spun and ran into him, pushing her off-balance.

He held her elbows to steady her. "Seeing each other is getting to be a habit."

Her blush showed to her roots, she was sure. "I'm usually pretty steady on my feet." No, actually she wasn't, but she didn't want to come off as a complete klutz.

"Except in those shoes."

His voice became so deep and quiet that the sound filled her soul. "Most men like women in high heels."

He studied her. "I'm not most men."

Those words slipped into her soul, covering it like ganache over a strawberry. She swallowed, but her mouth was a desert. "I'm thinking maybe you aren't."

He shuttered his eyes.

She took a breath; she licked her suddenly dry lips. She leaned into him with eyes closed. Instead of meeting his lips, she hit his nose. Didn't he want to kiss her? He'd been staring at her lips. She considered that action a universal sign.

"Ouch." He stepped back.

With some distance between them, she breathed a little easier. She'd misread the situation, and now she wished the ground swallowed her. "Oh, God, I'm sorry."

As he smiled, he held his nose. "I'm fine. You didn't hit me hard."

She could see his eyes were watering, so she must have hit him well. "Can I get you ice?"

He took a deep breath, then let go of his nose. "I'm fine. No blood."

"You sure? I'm so sorry." *He'll never want to try to kiss me again.*

This time, he took her head in his hands and guided her. He brushed his lips over hers, lightly at first.

A tingle danced up and down her spine. She grasped his shirt to pull him in closer. She thought she could be kissed any longer. He let go of her lips. He didn't release her head.

She mourned the loss of his warmth. Her body hummed with something undefinable, having never experienced a connection like that one with anyone. Paul was right there. He stared, a question in his eyes that she wasn't sure she could answer in words. He had done the right thing, and he could do that action again, if he wanted. "Wow." *That sounded so junior high.*

He grinned. "I'll take that as a compliment."

"Do."

He took his hand off of her head.

She mourned the loss of his touch.

He stared for a moment longer.

She did her best not to turn away. She'd never been kissed that way. Was the reason him or her feelings?

He offered an arm. "Shall we?"

She eyed the appendage. "I promise not to trip."

"Just a chivalrous gesture."

She laughed. The moment was gone, but not forgotten. "And I thought chivalry was dead." She could get lost in the tenderness she saw in his eyes.

"Not where I come from."

She took the proffered arm. "And where would that be?"

He hesitated.

Was he going to tell her a lie? She hoped not. Paul already seemed too good to be true.

"Bernardsville."

That answer made her eyebrows shoot up. Some of the richest people in the state lived in that town. The place was in an affluent area. Of course, they had mechanics, but she assumed those workers lived somewhere else. "Nice."

He pulled the car out and into the stream of traffic. "So, who is this Samuel guy?"

"A friend. Why do you ask?"

Paul glanced at her, then back to the road. "I'm wondering if he's competition."

He was serious. He wanted to know what was between her and Samuel. Would he understand their arrangement? Her breath hitched. "Uh, competition for what?"

"For you, silly. Do you think I'm hanging out with you because of your love of animals?"

"That is important to me."

"I realize that, but I like you, Daria. I enjoy your company."

She sighed. He'd said his feelings out loud. The thought of sharing her emotions scared her. "I'm not sure I'm very good company. I work long hours."

"Are you trying to shove me away?"

She bit her lip. She was pushing him away, even as she wanted to get closer to Paul. "I'm just laying out how things are."

"So, there are obstacles. Is Samuel one of them?"

What was Samuel? She didn't have a deep connection. He'd been hung up on Gloria for most of the year, and she'd been fine with his attention going in that direction. "He's a friend. We have a symbiotic relationship."

His turn signal clicked in the silence that followed.

He cleared his throat. "Symbiotic? That's very scientific. What do you mean?"

She took a deep breath, then let the air loose. "He needs a date for certain functions. I need to schmooze with rich people."

"Why?"

She shifted to look at him. "Why to which of those things I said?"

"Why do you need to network?"

"Because a shelter needs money. My vet practice doesn't take in enough to support the shelter part of my operation. So, I need an influx of cash, and some people need tax write-offs."

"Makes sense. There's nothing romantic between you?"

Why did Paul need to know?

Chapter Sixteen

With a light step, Paul opened Daria's car door. He'd driven to a restaurant for lunch. Daria needed money. He had money. He possessed a bushel of dollars, waiting for some worthy charity like one that rescues dogs and cats. He'd be done with his inheritance stipulations and the money would be in his bank in seven days.

Not only was she amazing to spend time with, but she was an answer to his dilemma. He had solved the problem and was having lunch with a beautiful woman. What could go wrong?

"Inside or out?" the greeter asked when they entered the restaurant situated on the Delaware River.

The day had dawned warm for this time of year, and Paul couldn't resist eating on the patio. "Outside okay?" he asked Daria.

Her smile shone brighter than the sun. "That sounds lovely."

They were seated at a table facing the river which flowed by slowly. A party boat sailed past them.

The people on the boat waved.

He couldn't help but wave back. Their glee was infectious, and he was a willing recipient.

The server handed them menus.

"Have you ever eaten here?" Daria asked.

"First time, but I've heard the food is good." When

they finished ordering, Paul decided to do some probing. "So, how much money do you need?"

She chuckled. "You plan on robbing a bank?"

He fidgeted with the napkin in his lap. "Not at all. I'm just curious."

A personal watercraft hummed past them.

She sighed. She rubbed her eyes. "The amount is so much that sometimes I'm overwhelmed thinking about it."

He moved his silverware around the table to give his hands something to do. "Have you figured out just what things would cost?"

"I have a spreadsheet."

How organized. She did have a handle on things. He could easily convince Jeeves her charity was a worthwhile one. "How can you know how much to ask for if you don't know how much you need?"

She cocked her head. "I just don't have the number memorized."

He could help the shelter. He'd created a business plan before he could get his first loan. "For instance, can you say how much the cost to house one dog for a day is?"

"No, but I could figure that out."

"Good. Then calculate that amount and you'll have a better idea of what you need."

She cocked her head. "The check from the couple at the benefit will cover renovations and additions. I've had estimates done on that."

"That's a start."

She slumped her shoulders. "A start, but the end seems so far away sometimes."

He put a hand on hers, noticing her soft skin.

"Other than financially, do you have a clear vision of what you want?"

"Yes, I do."

His mood brightened at the smile she gave him. She spoke of heated kennels and an operating room with play areas for each dog. He could almost buy into the dream, even if he wasn't fond of animals. Though Spike was wheedling his way into Paul's heart.

The food arrived. The burger he'd ordered made his mouth water while his stomach rumbled.

"Sounds like you have great plans. Now, eat so you don't pass out before you make those plans happen."

"Nothing is imminent." She put a bite of her salad in her mouth and then chewed. "Well, maybe the renovations."

Dishes clanked in the kitchen.

He decided to test the waters. He knew a lot of people and could help Daria in her quest. "I know a contractor. I can send him your way for another estimate."

She put down her fork and patted his hand. "Paul, you've done so much. I couldn't ask more."

He would do whatever he could to keep that smile. "Not a problem. Please. These animals are important to you."

She paused to study him.

He wondered if he'd said something wrong.

"Yes, the animals are. I'm not used to anyone other than Shelley's understanding."

He took a soft hand in his.

She smiled at their fingers intertwined.

"Samuel doesn't?" Paul asked.

As she released his hand, Daria laughed. "Not at

all. He'd sooner have a baby in his life as an animal. Hates them."

"Hates them? Maybe he was bitten as a child."

She widened her eyes. "You're defending him?"

Paul shrugged, taking a bite of a crisp French fry before he answered. "You never know why people don't like animals. He might never have been around them."

"That's possible. I never asked him." She laughed. "Isn't that silly?"

He shook his head. "You might never have been interested in his motives."

She bit her lip. "True. Do I even know yours?"

Paul considered himself a simple man. He liked to fix cars and make money doing it. Daria was the first woman who had ever caught his eye. He'd dated, but never seriously. "Mine are straightforward. I like you, Daria, and I enjoy spending time with you."

She blinked. "Cut to the chase, don't you?"

What would he say? He couldn't lie even more than he already was. Being dishonest would taint their relationship. "I'm a man who knows what I want."

She put a hand on her heart and widened her eyes. "And you want me?"

He chuckled. "Why do you sound as if you don't believe me?"

She rested her right elbow on the table and her chin on a hand. "I guess I do. I just don't understand why. Oh, it isn't that I don't know men find me attractive, I don't see that I have much to offer someone."

How could she say that? She was smart and beautiful and had the biggest heart of anyone he'd ever met. "What do you mean?"

She glanced at the river and then back. "I have big plans for my life. I haven't made room for a man."

Interesting. He was getting somewhere. "Is that why Samuel is so convenient?"

She put a hand on her chest. "Ouch. That hits close to home."

He shrugged. "Sorry. I call them how I see them."

"Yes, I see that." She stared at her food. "I have some cash now. In that case, you may send that contractor my way."

He smiled. Each step was Daria letting him get a little closer. His soul sang with the possibilities. "Why the change of heart?"

She cocked her head and eyed him. "Because for as long as you're here, I'll enjoy you all I can."

This woman had no idea how patient Paul could be. He worked on a car for months at a time. Wooing a woman was easy work compared to auto restoration. "You don't think I'll be around long."

"When you realize I won't have time to stroke your ego, you won't last."

He leaned back in the chair. "Is that what has happened in the past?"

"At times."

He leaned closer. "Honey, my ego is big enough which means you don't need to stroke it." Would she believe him?

****

Daria dutifully bought a present and showed up at the address given for the biggest house she'd ever seen. So this was how her sisters lived. Long white columns adorned a front porch. The large windows dotted the façade. As far as she could tell, the place had a third floor. Her cottage would probably fit into the foyer of this McMansion.

The skies above threatened to rain, but the precipitation had held off so far.

Someone had been christened today.

Daria couldn't make it to the church, but Carmela had invited her back to the house. Daria figured now was as good a time as any to meet the family. She stood in front of the oak door with a brass knocker, wondering if she could back out. She could smell steaks on a grill. She gulped. "Once again, I get to be outclassed."

Glancing down at her big box store slacks and thrift store blouse, she hoped she didn't stand out too much. At least rain wasn't falling, and she could wear sensible shoes. She rang the doorbell, chiming the "1812 Overture." *Really?* Some part of her wanted to run away. She didn't belong here, and everyone must know. She wiped her palms on her slacks.

The door swung open.

Music spilled out as did the sounds of chatter pushing her a step back. The noise alone made her pause.

Someone squealed her name from farther into the giant house.

Carmela?

The man who opened the door held out a hand. He stood well over six feet tall with long limbs. "Come in. I'll take the present."

She proffered the gift. "Thanks."

"I'm Jerry Loschiavo. A cousin of yours. My father and Uncle Mario are brothers." He smiled.

She smiled. "Nice to meet you." The afternoon was

headed in a direction she wasn't comfortable with. Like a family reunion, they would all be figuring out how they were related. She'd never remember them all.

Carmela appeared.

She must have been the one who squealed.

Carmela motioned to the man who had taken the present. "Daria, you've met Jerry. Come in. There are more to meet."

Daria stayed still. She could see throngs of people. What would she say? Did she have anything in common with them other than blood? *Hi, I'm Mario's illegitimate daughter.* Daria's breath left. "Coming here was a mistake."

Would she ever fit in with this family?

****

After the christening, Daria sat on the couch with her emotions on a rollercoaster. She couldn't remember anyone's name. She practically spun from being with that number of people all at once, and she couldn't get comfortable with all the food she'd eaten.

Carmela had warned her about more family events. How did they get together so often and not go crazy? How did they keep track of each other? She wanted to shut down and start again tomorrow.

She glanced at her phone. Paul had left a message. She wasn't ready to deal with him, either. He made her head spin. She'd had no time to recover from the forthright pronouncement of his ego not needing to be stroked. He wouldn't last long, no matter what he said. She did not have room in life for a relationship now. With the check from the Gaudettes, she could renovate. Then she could house more animals.

Her phone ringing interrupted her thoughts. Not

having many friends who called, the noise startled her out of her thoughts. "Hello?"

"Ms. Jacks?"

"Yes." She hoped the caller wasn't a shelter. She didn't have room. Besides, she had no transportation and bothering Shelley was not an option. Sunday was family day at Shelley's house.

"This is Gino Giammetti. I'm a friend of Pauly Vincenzo. He said you were searching for a contractor."

A contractor calling on a Sunday? "Yes, I am. I have some renovations and additions to be done in my vet's office. Well, the building next door."

"I could come out tomorrow around nine in the morning and take a look."

"Okay." Not wanting to get her hopes up, she took a deep breath. Contractors had the reputation of overpromising and underdelivering. She didn't want to get caught in that whirlwind, so she didn't make any plans.

"I'll see you tomorrow, then."

"Mr. Giammetti, do you need directions?"

"No, ma'am. Pauly gave them to me."

The man disconnected. *Pauly?* Who was he, and how had he come into her life? "I wish I had connections to find out who people are. Pauly?"

Well, she did. She just hated to rely on Mario. Should she take him at face value?

Chapter Seventeen

Paul and Jeeves stood outside the kitchen of the big house. The patio had an awning that shielded them from the sun during midday, but not at the moment.

"So, how do I train him?" Paul asked.

Spike was still leashed. He sat staring at Jeeves, his eyes wide and his tongue hanging out of the side of his mouth.

His dog's reverence for Jeeves sat on Paul like an itchy sweater. He'd be the one who'd saved him that rainy night. He'd be the one who had cleaned the dog's vomit and made him poached chicken. He raised his face to the warm sun, hoping for inspiration.

The leaves on the trees were thinking about changing color, and the air held a crispness that reminded him of Granny Smith apples. Someone close by was burning leaves.

Jeeves handed him the tome. "I bought you a book."

"Have you trained a dog before?"

Jeeves snorted. "I've told you."

Paul eyed Jeeves. "Right. Butlers to royalty."

Jeeves shook his head and then spun to enter the kitchen.

"Where are you going?"

He hated the desperation in his voice. Give him a nice 302 cubic inch engine with a four-barrel, and he could make the motor sing. People were another matter, and dogs were foreign.

"Read the book." Jeeves closed the door behind him.

Paul swiveled back to the dog who sat with his tongue hanging out. "At least today, it isn't raining."

The dog trotted over.

"Sit."

The dog's rump went down.

"So, you are trained. You just won't listen."

The dog licked his outstretched hand.

"Stay."

He stepped backward twice.

The dog followed.

"Sit. Stay."

The dog sat.

Paul once again stepped away.

The dog followed again but sat at his feet.

"Maybe we need to work on something else." He scratched his chin. "You know sit. Give me your paw."

Spike raised a paw.

That action made Paul laugh. Whoever had owned Spike had trained him to do some things. "Okay."

Jeeves opened the door and handed out a box.

He took the box with a picture of a dog on the front. He hated when Jeeves was cryptic. "What's this?"

Jeeves eyed him over half-glasses. "Treats. Dogs will do anything for food."

Paul set the box on a bench. Taking one out, he showed the treat to Spike. "Stay."

This time, the dog stayed.

"Now, come."

The dog trotted over, taking the treat.

"Good dog." He patted the dog's head.

When Spike finished the biscuit, he rubbed his head against Paul's knee.

They were becoming friends at least. He sighed. The more time he spent with Spike, the less likely he'd give him back. "That was good. Can you play dead?"

The dog lay down and then rolled onto his back.

He laughed and handed the dog two treats. "You're good."

Jeeves studied them from the door. "He must belong to someone."

Paul hadn't thought about someone actually owning the dog. Someone could be missing their pet. "I think you're right. I really better put signs up."

"That would be the right thing to do."

He captured Jeeves' gaze. "Did I tell you I've found a place for that money?"

"Really. And you can donate anonymously?" Jeeves crossed his arms.

He had the final say on where the money ended up. He might be a tough sell. "I want to donate the money to Daria's shelter. She can save a lot of dogs."

"I didn't know you were interested in dogs. That is part of the stipulation. This donation needs to be a gift from the heart."

Paul put his hands on his hips. "So, what do I have to do to prove that this donation is from my heart?"

He paused for a moment. "If you don't find the owner, keep Spike."

Spike stared at Paul.

He gazed at the dog, to Jeeves, and back to the dog. "I feel like I'm being ganged up on."

"You want your inheritance?"

"I guess I do. Okay, I'll hang the signs near where I found him."

"What if your lady friend sees?"

Paul hoped she wouldn't.

****

Daria glanced at her watch while leaning against the lobby counter. The contractor showed up five minutes late to the meeting with Daria. And he apologized for his tardiness. As she stood in the lobby, she didn't know what to say.

Gino Giammetti was a large man in every sense. His legs were tree trunks, and his arms were the branches. Three counties over could hear that voice.

The dogs in the back barked.

He had a twinkle in his brown eyes and an easy smile.

Daria decided she liked him and hoped he gave the best price. As she spoke, she walked him around the building. "I need the building expanded by two thousand feet. I'll need a place to wash dogs." She explained more about what she wanted.

He repeated her plans back and then wrote down a price on a piece of paper.

The amount made her jaw drop. She'd gotten a few estimates, but she hadn't had the money, so she never called anyone back. "Your price is one thousand dollars cheaper than anyone else."

Gino shrugged. "A friend of Pauly's is a friend of mine."

He kept his gaze on her.

She couldn't detect a lie in anything he said. Should she try for another contractor to be sure? "Okay.

I'll get back to you, then."

"I have a break in my schedule early next week. If you let me know this week, then I can order materials and have them delivered before I get here."

"That sounds great, but I haven't signed the lease on the building yet."

He shook her right hand with his beefy one. "Have a nice day, Miss Jacks."

"Who the heck was that?" Shelley asked.

"A friend of Paul's. A contractor." She stared at the paper with his price. "He gave me a great estimate. I'm not sure if I can trust him."

Shelley snatched the paper. She whistled. "You can't afford *not* to take this offer."

Things couldn't be this easy. "But what personal cost do I pay?"

She rolled her eyes. "Gee, you might have just found a great guy. That would be a horrible personal cost to you."

Daria didn't answer.

Shelley snorted. "The terrier is first."

She took in the waiting room filled with two dogs and a cat in a container. "I should get the cat through first. The dogs like each other."

As she checked over the cat, a blue point Siamese, she mulled over Gino's estimate. He'd called her on a Sunday. He'd come almost on time. This punctuality was not normal behavior for a contractor. She'd had estimates from three others. They'd all acted like they were doing her a favor. "Nikki will be fine. She's doing great for eighteen years old."

The owner smiled and put the cat back in the container.

Shelley poked her head into the exam room. "Paul's on the phone."

"You should take a message.'

"He said he really wants to talk to you, and he might not get another break today."

Daria frowned. "I'll take the call in my office." As she passed through the lobby, she motioned to the dog owners. "I have to take this call, then I'll be right with you."

She settled herself in her chair and then picked up the receiver. "Hello?"

"Daria. Did Gino come by?"

She settled her butt on the edge of the desk. "What do you have on him?

"What do you mean?"

"He called me on Sunday, presumably after you spoke. He came five minutes late and apologized, then he gave me a quote a lot cheaper than anyone else."

"What's wrong with that?"

She settled on the office chair. "Paul, I've had three contractors in here. All with attitudes."

"Was he polite?"

"He was more than polite? He was charming." Unexpected was another word she would use to describe Gino. He'd been refreshingly honest.

"I hope not too charming."

Was Paul jealous? She laughed. "No. The point is I don't feel I can trust the offer. Are there strings attached."

"Strings? From me?"

"Yes, like if you decide to get lost, he will, too."

"I won't decide to get lost, and neither will he. Just trust me, Daria."

Could she trust him?

****

When she visited Dad this time, Daria had Gino's card. Maybe she would get used to the place. Mario'd know if he was crooked or not. She still flinched at the clank of the gate and recoiled at the antiseptic scent. The smell lingered for hours. She put the card on the table, pulled out the chair, and sat.

The guard glanced at the card and shrugged.

She had no intention of leaving anything with Mario.

"Gino Giammetti."

"One of yours?" she asked.

"No, he's clean. He doing the shelter for you?"

Daria leaned back in her seat. She'd hoped that Gino was clean. She'd liked him and liked his shelter design. "Yep, at a great price."

Dad picked up the card, turning over the colorful paper. "Good price. I could get you better."

Dad's involvement was the last thing she wanted. Far too many strings would be attached to anything Mario did. She shook her head. "No. Absolutely not."

"Independent, huh?"

She narrowed her eyes. "Yes. You are not helping with my plans."

Grabbing the card, she snagged him with her nail. "Ouch."

Daria winced. "Sorry."

"Clumsy." Dad examined his hand. "I'll live."

But would she make it through these visits?

Chapter Eighteen

Paul posted signs on telephone poles where he had found Spike. One sign he hung on the post near the diner where he and Daria had their first meal. Would she see it? If she did, the situation would be a sign in more ways than one. Cars rushed past him on the busy road.

At least it wasn't raining. As he placed the last sign on a pole, he squinted up at the sun. He shook his head. "I can't deceive her any longer." With his path sure, he climbed back into the car and drove to her office.

No one sat in the waiting room, so Shelley waved him back.

Daria hunched over paperwork.

He leaned on the doorway, watching her tucking hair behind her ears which refused to stay. The place was the quietest he'd ever heard with no dogs barking. He paused, enjoying the sight of her tongue peeking out of her mouth. What did the future hold for them? He had no idea, and he didn't relish the conversation ahead. Would she be disappointed? "Hey."

She jumped and put a hand over her heart. "Jeez, Paul. You scared me."

He sat across from her. "Not my intention."

She began to rise. "What brings you here? Is Spike okay?"

Paul waved her back into her seat. "Yes, he's fine.

I need to talk to you."

"This conversation couldn't wait?"

"No, I've needed to talk to you for days."

She put down her pen and then settled back in the leather chair. "Go ahead." She scrunched her face and then gripped the chair's arms.

Before he could speak, Shelley poked her head in. "We have an emergency coming in. Dog hit by a car."

Daria catapulted out of the chair. "This conversation has to wait."

When he truly wanted to come clean and couldn't, he sat for a moment more frustrated. Because he wanted to get closer to Daria, he'd kept the dog.

She wouldn't be happy. Would he?

****

Shelley, Paul, and Daria sat in Daria's office after the emergency was over. Her adrenaline had long ago left, and she couldn't move. She had two more patients for the day. Her strength had to come back, so she popped open a soda for a caffeine jolt.

"Don't you have a job, Paul, or are you independently wealthy?" Shelley asked.

He coughed and looked around.

The question must have struck close to the truth. Daria wanted to know the answer also. He made his own hours and not many. "And when will my car be done?" Daria asked.

He smiled at the two women. "Tomorrow when I get the part. I run my own car repair business, and I don't have any projects. Besides, I had an errand and needed to talk to Daria."

"I get the hint." She left.

Exhaustion seeped into Daria's bones. The caffeine

didn't help. She rubbed her eyes. "So, what is so important that you needed to see me in the middle of the day?"

He shook his head. "You're tired. This conversation can wait." He stood. "I'd better go."

As if he were marking his territory, before he left, he kissed her. As much as she hated the idea, she liked the idea. She wasn't something to be marked, but if she was, she'd like Paul to mark her. Was he willing?

****

Paul sat on the large staircase in the two-story foyer of the big house. "Jeeves, we need to make that donation." He had slid down the banister more than once the foyer was his favorite room in the house

Jeeves paused from dusting the front hall. He held a duster still. "Oh? What's made you so sure?"

Daria in a word, but Jeeves needed more than that simple explanation. He'd experienced something today that he'd never before. Lending a hand with that animal opened a piece of his heart he didn't know had been closed. "I assisted Daria work on a hurt dog today. I had so much satisfaction in helping this little animal." Paul finally had some appreciation of why she did what she did. He understood the importance of saving the animals.

"Will you feel this way tomorrow?"

Yes, and he didn't want Jeeves to question this feeling. "Jeeves, don't rain on my decision. I'm sure giving the money to Daria is what I want. Make the donation happen."

"I'll think about it."

He wanted to slap his head. He didn't require the inheritance; he just didn't like things hanging over him.

He also disliked that he hadn't told Daria the truth. Spike lay at Paul's feet wherever he settled, so maybe the dog had chosen him. "I am keeping you. We just need to set some ground rules."

Jeeves grinned. "Ground rules?"

"Yes, like where he can sleep. I've got to figure out what he can and can't eat."

"He needs a walk right now."

Paul looked from Jeeves to the dog and then back. "He tells you that?"

Jeeves stared at the dog. "I just know."

So, he took the dog outside.

A rabbit crossed their paths.

Spike took off in pursuit.

He had to let the leash go and trotted behind to keep the dog in sight. His phone rang. He stopped to answer the call and lost Spike in the woods. "Damn."

"Hey, Pauly, that's no way to answer the phone."

He laughed. "Sorry, Gino. I lost my dog."

"I didn't know you had a dog."

Paul looked in every direction for the dog. "Recent acquisition."

"Has your lady friend made a decision? I have another job I can schedule if she isn't going with me."

He ran a hand through his hair. "You just talked to her this morning."

"I know, but this other job came up."

He rubbed his chin. He'd forgotten to shave that morning. "I asked you for a favor, Gino."

"I know. I know. Okay, I won't schedule anything until I hear from her. Hey, that's one fine lady. What's she doing with you?"

Paul wondered that turn of events himself, but he

wouldn't question her out loud. "I'm not sure she is with me."

"Then you better make sure. Women like that don't sit around."

Paul disconnected, calling for Spike. He found him outside the repair garage, his teeth in a plastic jug. "Spike. No. Antifreeze is poison."

****

Paul drove like an ambulance with lights and siren on. He just stopped for red lights. Antifreeze was poison for dogs, but he didn't know how badly Spike was doing.

Spike wasn't showing any signs of poisoning. Instead, he was hopping between the front seat and the back seat. Sometimes, he'd lick him on the face. Other times, he stuck his head by the partially opened window.

"Damn. You don't look sick. Daria said to bring you in." So, here he was racing to her office. That moment was when he decided he was keeping Spike. He couldn't imagine life without the dog now. The little animal was embedded in his heart.

Dad wanted him to think outside himself. His request made sense now. "It's too funny that something Dad hated will make me into the person he wanted me to be." He pulled into Daria's parking lot, not bothering to turn off the engine. He yanked Spike behind him. "Excuse me," he said to a lady with a poodle on the path to the front door.

She looked over him. Then she recognized him. "Pauly Vincenzo."

"Hello, Mrs. Radfield. Spike's sick."

Paul hoped Mrs. Radfield wouldn't mention how

he knew her.

****

Daria dropped the phone onto the receiver. Time was of the essence, and if they didn't have what was needed, she would redirect Paul to another vet. "Shelley, track down that antidote for antifreeze."

"Okay," she called from the other room. "It was on a back order, and I don't know if it came in yet.

Daria's pulse quickened. If Spike hadn't ingested too much, this intervention would go smoothly. She waited, pacing.

The pair breezed in half an hour later.

"His coat is dull and his eye aren't bright."

The gravity of the situation had darkened the color of his widened eyes. "Is antifreeze bad?"

"Poison. Get him into the back. We need to do a stomach lavage and administer the antidote."

Shelley had found their one batch of the medicine in the storeroom.

Daria had never been so relieved.

Paul did as she said.

Daria met him in the back with Shelley. Concern was evident in his knitted brow. "You might want to wait outside."

He shook his head. "I'll stay."

"Stay back then."

"Daria, please save him."

Could she save this dog?

****

Two hours later, Spike rested comfortably in a cage in the back room.

Paul sat across Daria's desk from her. Lines creased her face. Exhaustion slumped her shoulders.

His posture mirrored hers. Over a dog. A dog that had wormed its way into his heart. "What now?"

"We'll do a blood test in the morning to see if there is any trace of the antifreeze in his system." Her words came out with effort.

He pinched his nose, thinking he shouldn't have taken that phone call. "He got loose from me."

She put up a hand. "I don't think his poisoning happened intentionally, but maybe you have to be more careful with your stuff."

He nodded. Guilt racked him, sapping his strength. He was just starting to like Spike. He didn't want to lose him now. "I will. Before he comes home. Can you give me a list of things dangerous to dogs?" He sighed. Now would be a good time to come clean. No. He would keep Spike if his owner wasn't found, but he had to try to find that owner.

She rose. "I'm wiped and need a shower. Can I kick you out?"

"That's fine." He stood and took her hands. "Let me know if anything changes."

"Sure."

He took her in his arms and left a sweet kiss on her cheek. He needed to come clean about the dog soon.

Chapter Nineteen

After a shower and a nap at home, Daria realized her stomach grumbled for dinner. Since she didn't have her car, she still hadn't gone shopping. With the refrigerator empty, the diner would have to do. She called in her order ahead of time.

The day had ended as pleasant as it began weather-wise. She strolled the one block to what was rapidly becoming a regular haunt.

The sun was settling onto the horizon.

Someone had tacked posters on the telephone pole. They had found a black dog.

Daria stopped to read the sign.

The dog reminded her of Spike. The phone number was Paul's. She puzzled over that coincidence for a moment. What could the sign mean? Then everything became clear. He wasn't keeping Spike.

He'd lied. Fury propelled her feet to the diner to get the food. As she was not fit for the company, she asked for the food to be wrapped up to go. When she arrived home, she hit speed dial to call Shelley. "He lied to me."

"Who?"

She paced in her living room. Three steps one way, three steps the other, digging her toes into the carpeting. "Paul. He isn't keeping Spike."

"How do you know he isn't keeping Spike? Calm

down."

She hurt at the memory. "I saw a sign for a dog on the telephone pole by the diner. The sign had Paul's phone number."

"Oh. I'm not sure I can think of a valid explanation."

She wasn't interested in an explanation. She shook her head, then remembered that Shelley couldn't see her. "I can. He lied."

"Why?"

Her head of steam faltered for a moment. "I haven't figured that far. I can't see straight because of how furious I am. He charmed me. Moved in for the kill. He even schmoozed me with his contactor friend."

Shelly cleared her throat. "Why don't you call him? Maybe he has a reasonable explanation."

She slapped a hand on her chest to stop the pain. "I don't ever want to see him again."

"He deserves a chance."

"Why?"

"Because he's the only man in your life who doesn't mock your need to help animals. Samuel makes a joke of your passion."

She had a point, but not one Daria wanted to take. "I need to calm down first."

"Yes, good idea. Have you had dinner?"

She couldn't think about eating right now.

****

Paul stood in the shop with his phone in his hand. . He'd been putting away his tools for the day. Paul could feel Daria's fury even before she told him what she was mad at. He'd been found out. Her anger hurtled through the phone. He still had the paper from the doctor who confirmed what he'd thought.

Leftover rain dripped off the roof, but the sun had come out.

"I saw the sign. You want to tell me the truth for once."

"I'm sorry, Daria. I've been meaning to tell you, but. . ."

"But what? You don't know what the truth is?"

He deserved that accusation. She had talked about honesty a lot. Even Samuel, with all his faults, had always been honest. Paul'd committed the cardinal sin. "I tried yesterday, but then you had an emergency. Then I tried today, but you kicked me out."

"So, your deception is my fault?"

He cringed. Those words sounded like an excuse. She was right to call him on it. "No, that's not what I'm saying. I had to work up the courage."

"I'm a monster then?"

He wanted to crawl through the phone and talk. She couldn't see that he was sorry for not being more forthright. "No, Daria, but your heart is on your sleeve about animals. I didn't want to hurt you. I didn't want you to think less of me if I couldn't keep Spike."

"You already did. So, tell me the story. The real story."

"I found out I'm allergic to dogs. I can't keep Spike.

"Why didn't you tell me?"

"Because you told me how awful things would be for him to go back to a shelter. Even yours. I couldn't do that. Jeeves insisted that I find his former owner."

"So, you aren't keeping him?"

He sighed. He wished things were different. "I

don't think I can, Daria. I've been pretty sick with him here."

"I need some time to think about this situation. I don't want to see you."

She wasn't being fair, but he had kept things from her, so no need to point out that fact. "Okay. When I finish your car, I'll have someone else drop the vehicle off. Tomorrow."

"Fine."

The dial tone startled him.

****

The next day, a tall man with olive skin and a British accent handed Daria the keys.

As he held himself tall, his imposing presence filled the lobby. The man couldn't be unobtrusive if he tried. He smelled of vanilla. "Thank you." She stared. "Who are you?"

"Jeeves, Miss Jacks."

That name didn't tell her anything. She took in his formal attire. "You don't look like a friend of Paul's." Then again, what did she know about him? How could she tell if someone was a friend or not?

"I'm his butler."

"Butler?" Daria laughed. What was a mechanic doing with a butler? "That's what I'd have pegged you for."

He bowed, a small smile on his face. "I'll take that as a compliment."

"Do." Daria shook her head. Paul was full of surprises. She wasn't sure she liked any of them. "Well, thank you for bringing my car back."

"If I may have a word?"

She was game. What did she have to lose? "Yes?"

He glanced around at the owners with dogs and cats in the lobby. "In private."

"Come back to my office." When they reached the room, she motioned. "Sit."

He didn't shrug, just stayed motionless. "I'll stand."

"I'm hurting my neck staring at you."

He was taller than Paul. He sat on the edge of the seat. "First, how is Spike?"

"He's fine. No trace of antifreeze in his system."

"Can he come home?"

The accent made her smile. "Not yet. I want to give him another day of IV fluids, just to be sure."

Jeeves nodded. "Pauly's a good kid."

Pauly? Oh, Paul. Why did everyone call him that version of his name? "Did he send you here?"

"No. He'd be mad if he knew."

She folded her hands in her lap. "Then why come here and risk getting fired?"

A slight grin creased his face. "He can't fire me."

"I'm not interested in hearing that Paul was a Boy Scout."

He smiled and shook his head. "He wasn't. But I have seen a change in him. He was genuinely worried about Spike. Before now and you, he didn't even like animals."

"Is he keeping Spike?"

"Yes, he's already rearranged his garage, so all the dangerous things are up high. He's even decided to go for allergy shots. If he doesn't find the owner, he'll do his best for Spike."

She tapped a pen on her desk, wondering what this man's angle was. "Good. Otherwise I probably wouldn't let him have Spike back."

He raised his eyebrows. "You could do that?"

She shrugged. "I could try."

"Then don't. He'll take good care of Spike."

"Fine. That's all I need to know." She stood, signaling the conversation was over. She didn't need to hear anymore about Pauly. He was already too close to her heart.

"You don't want to hear what else I have to say in Pauly's defense?"

She'd heard quite enough about a guy she didn't want to be interested in.

****

On Daria's phone that night, Gino's number appeared. She'd settled with dinner on her flowered couch, but she had to answer the phone. She needed to know where she stood. "Your offer is still in effect, regardless of my relationship with Paul?" She gripped the warm plate, waiting for an answer.

"Yes, I keep my word."

She bit her lip. How close was this guy to Paul? Would she see Paul at all? "Seeing as you are the best offer, I'll take it."

"We can start whenever you like. The construction will take a month."

Yeah, right, but she didn't argue. But she still hadn't signed the lease, and the sign for Vinny's Weenies still mocked her. After she hung up, a knock sounded on her door. Gazing through the peephole, she saw a young kid holding a basket. She opened the door.

"Daria Jacks?"

"Yes."

"Delivery."

She took the basket, placing the container on the table by the door. She found a few dollars and handed them to the delivery boy.

He tipped his hat and then left.

Without really wanting to, she sniffed the flowers. They smelled of summertime and promises. The card told her they were from Paul. She rolled her eyes. She'd talked to him just yesterday. Less than twenty-four hours wasn't enough time. She called him anyway. Might as well get this call over with. She paced in her living room. "You said you'd give me space."

"I did. I just wanted to remind you I'm still here. Can I take Spike home?"

"You still want to?"

"Certainly. Jeeves gave me the good news. I have some medication until the allergy shots kick in."

She settled back on the couch. As much as she wanted space from Paul, she did enjoy hearing his voice. "Yes, I met your, uh, butler."

A chuckle came through the phone. "What'd you think?"

She thought back to the tall, olive-skinned man who had been in the office. "He had an air about him, but something in his eyes spoke of the streets."

"Not far off. He's pulled himself up by his bootstraps."

"I'm sure I don't want to know why he's your butler."

"Probably not at this point. I'll tell you everything, if you'll let me."

She shifted in the chair. "No more plants. No more flowers."

"Okay."

He sounded like a little kid who'd been reprimanded.

He said his goodbyes.

Daria was reluctant to let him get off the phone. Would he call her again despite her pleas?

Chapter Twenty

Carmela, and the rest of the Loschiavo clan, including Daria, sat in the visitor's room at the jail. Daria pulled her sweater closer around her. Families were murmuring all around them.

"My heart is full," Mario Loschiavo said, his smile full. "To see all my children together."

Daria had originally balked at the idea, but these people were family. Warts and all, she had a family now, even if she needed more time to get used to them.

Each one sat on a metal chair that hadn't been designed for comfort.

He wanted them all together before the trial.

Daria still hadn't decided to sit with them or even attend the trial.

Mario still swore he was innocent.

A big part of Daria wanted to believe him. Daria glanced at Maria and Carmela. The family gathering had been tough, but she'd been welcomed warmly. She had a family. She'd never thought she'd wanted a family.

"Daddy, we're so glad you made us go see Daria," said Carmela.

Would Daria ever get used to the idea?

****

Paul's chances were good now. Something in Daria's voice when she'd called about the flowers made him think he had a chance. But first, he had to deal with the donation. As usual, he found Jeeves in the kitchen. The man dominated this part of the house. "Let's do the donation."

"What?"

He stalked through the kitchen to the refrigerator. He pulled out a bottle of water and then twisted it open. "Give the money to Daria's place."

Jeeves smiled. "I'm glad, Pauly. Now, you just have to win her back."

That situation was another problem, but the first one, the will, hung over his head. Once he donated the money, then he could concentrate on Daria. "At least, the donation will be anonymous."

Jeeves eyed him. "Why would that be a problem any other way?"

"Because if she knew the donor was me, she'd think I was giving the money to get her back."

Jeeves put down the newspaper. "I see. Will she get the whole amount?"

"Yes. Her ideals are close to my heart, and she won't squander the money."

Jeeves nodded, a smile erupting on his usually taciturn face. "You've learned a lot in a short time."

"I had a good teacher. How about I take you out to dinner, Jeeves?"

"Me and you out to dinner? Sorry, I have a date."

He didn't know the man dated. "You old rascal. Good for you. Have fun. Can you pick up Spike for me tomorrow?"

"You don't want to chance seeing Daria?"

Paul wanted to see Daria, but did she want to see him?

****

Shelley ran into Daria's office. "You are not gonna believe what I just opened. Look at this mail."

Daria, who sat behind her desk, a folder on top, took the letter and the check. "What's wrong?" She read the letter, swiveling the chair back and forth. The arrival of the check was too coincidental to think it wasn't a trap. Or something worse.

As she stood in the doorway, Shelley vibrated. "We've been chosen as a benefactor of an anonymous donor."

Frowning, Daria shook her head. "I don't like this situation."

Shelley's excitement rolled off of her. "What is not to like about a number with that many zeroes?"

Daria was always suspicious of something that seemed too good to be true. She tugged at her lab coat sleeves. "Who would give this much money to us? What do they want in return?"

She planted her bottom on the edge of the desk. "You are so suspicious."

"And my instincts have gotten me out of a lot of messes." Daria dropped the check on the desk. This situation was too good to be true. Someone wanted something, and she needed to find out what before she cashed this check. "What's the return address?"

"United Charities. They specialize in anonymous donors. People who want to give, but not make a big deal. They would have checked out this guy."

Guy? She narrowed her eyes. Could this money be from Mario? "Who says the donor is a guy?"

Shelley waved her hand. "Girl, whatever."

Daria bit her lip. She wasn't one to peer into a gift

horse's mouth, but this charity didn't sit right. "This check will probably bounce."

She rolled her eyes. "I'd run to the bank before this person changes their mind."

"Call United Charities and see if they'll tell us who gave this money. Tell them we won't cash the check until we know who this check is from."

Shelley frowned. "You're cold."

She waved her hand. "And calculating. I'm just protecting my animals."

Shelley stood, shrugged, then took back the check. "You don't have a romantic bone in your body."

"Nope, had the romance removed with my appendix."

Shelley humphed and then flounced out of the room. She strode back in. "I'll make you call them. I refuse."

Did Shelley have the right attitude about the check?

****

Daria paused before she entered the visiting room at the prison. Sweat poured down her back as if someone had turned on the heat too high. The place wasn't any more charming than the first time she'd been here. The green walls reminded her of an old hospital.

Mario smiled.

Too bad he still wasn't ready to treat him like a parent. What was he in her life? She was all grown and didn't need a parent. He hadn't been present for the important dates. She wasn't ready to forgive even if his absence wasn't his fault, completely.

"Hello, Daria."

"Hello." She sat across from him folding her hands on the cold metal table.

Mario leaned his elbows on that table. "I have something to tell you."

She wasn't sure she could handle any more news today. "Oh?"

He wiped a hand down his face. "You have a fund. I guess a trust fund."

Why was he telling her about the fund right now? "Okay."

"The account has your name on it. No one knew I was putting that money aside"

She didn't know what to say. "I, uh, why?"

He tugged at the sleeves of his jumpsuit, and he then flattened his hands on the table. "Because once I knew you existed, then I had to take care of you. And here you want to do some good in the world. Carmela and Maria will probably not make an impact. I spoiled them. My fault."

She drummed her fingers. "I can't accept the money."

"Why not?"

She shook her head. "Because this money is dirty. You did illegal things to make that money."

He didn't argue, and that reaction made things worse. Part of her wanted Mario to be a good man. She wanted the charges against him to be bogus. She hadn't been sure until that moment, and now butterflies were in her stomach.

"You could do something good with those dollars. Make the cash clean again."

She stood. She couldn't listen anymore. "No, I don't want your money."

Mario called her name.

Daria paused a moment before she left the prison. The flashbulb going off made her wish she'd stayed home today.

****

Daria's car sat outside of her clinic, and she eyed the vehicle. She blinked in the bright sun.

Paul needed to check she was happy with her car. He couldn't wait to see what she had to say. The day was perfect for a drive in the sports car. He doubted that she did anything that whimsical ever. Money wasted on gas couldn't go to the animals.

He meandered around the car in silence.

She frowned, resting her hands on her hips. "Right now is the first chance I've had to look at it. Why'd you do it?"

"Do what?"

She touched where he'd done some work on the exterior. "Touch up the paint."

He stopped. With hesitation, he took her right hand in his. "Because I have a soft spot for redheads or a certain one, and I have a soft spot for pony cars. I couldn't let the car live out its days with a dodgy paint job."

She studied her right hand in his.

He hoped he reminded her sufficiently of a puppy to sway her anger.

She sighed, squeezing his hand. "Thank you. The car does look so much better."

He blew out a breath he'd been holding. He held her face. "I'm glad you like it."

She nodded.

He leaned in to kiss her. He couldn't believe she let

him. He'd be walking on air for the rest of the day.

****

Paul left Daria in the office all warm and fuzzy. The sensation wrapped around her like a blanket. He was a great guy, and she was lucky to have him. Then the reality of the check from United Charities crashed down. She didn't want to make this call but had to. She was wired. Some part of her wanted this check to be real. She tapped her phone. While the device rang, she waited.

"United Charities," a perky, young woman answered.

"Hi. I'm Doctor Daria Jacks. I received a donation for my animal shelter through United Charities, and I want to know who donated the money." A silence ensued only a deaf person couldn't hear.

"But that's the point, ma'am. Our donors want to stay anonymous."

Frustration snaked down her spine. Could she explain herself well enough that this woman would understand? She didn't convince Shelley. "Why? Why would someone want to give a large amount of money and not get some kind of credit for the donation?"

The girl on the phone paused.

She probably had a script. Daria was deviating from it.

"They can take a tax deduction."

She tucked her leg underneath her, settling in to find the answer. "But this amount is a lot of money. Like political campaign money where someone gets something in return."

"I'm not sure I understand. Let me get my supervisor. Hold on."

Symphony music filtered down the line, then it stopped abruptly. "This is Mildred Gluck. How can I help you?"

Daria, once again, explained her story.

The woman sighed. "What I can do is contact that donor and see if that person will reconsider his or her anonymity. I haven't had this request before." The woman paused. "So, you're afraid of who might have given this money?"

That's exactly what Daria was afraid of.

Chapter Twenty-One

Later that day, Daria settled with coffee and a newspaper in her office. She had no appointments for a whole thirty minutes. The squeak in the chair reminded her to oil it. She smelled popcorn and wished Shelley brought her some.

She wasn't settled for long. On the society page of the paper was a large photo of her. She'd been leaving the courthouse with her sunglasses on. The reporter recognized her, anyway. "Oh, heck."

She'd just gotten used to the idea of being the daughter of the head of a famous family. How did they figure out which person she was visiting? This situation wasn't good and might reflect badly on the plans for a shelter. Who was she kidding? This photo could reflect badly on her practice.

She dialed Mario's lawyer. He had given the number the last time she visited him. "As much as this development pains me, I need your help. Have you seen the paper?"

He chuckled. "Yes, the reporter paid off a guard to tip him off."

She rubbed a hand down her face. "Can we do anything?"

The lawyer cleared his throat. "Of course, but seems to me you would want this story to die quickly."

He wasn't wrong. She'd rather this story stayed

buried on a back page. She didn't want reporters or even gawkers disrupting her life. "What do you think I should do?"

"Go about your day as if you have no idea someone took this picture. And don't visit Mario for a while. I'll let him know."

She hung up. The phone rang a second later. She didn't answer. Instead, she switched off the ringer. Anyone in her circle would call her cell.

Besides, she had a decision to make.

****

Paul wiped his hands on a rag before he answered the ringing cell phone. The car in front of him would have to wait. His focus hadn't been on work all morning, and he hoped this call wouldn't make things worse. He had the garage door open because a nice breeze was blowing through it.

"This is Mildred Gluck from United Charities. I wanted to speak to Paul Vincenzo."

"That's me. What can I do for you?" He leaned against the current project, a 1966 pony car. She wasn't rusted but had many dents and dings. The inside reminded him of a crime scene. He would send it out for the upholstery to be done because that skill wasn't in his wheelhouse.

"You donated to the Happy Valley Animal Shelter."

Uh oh. He pushed away from the car and walked around it. His chest tightened. "Yes, I did. Is there a problem?"

"The person who runs that, Daria Jacks, says she will not cash the check unless she knows who the donor is."

He sighed. Being anonymous was the strictest stipulation. He rubbed a hand down his face. "I was assured complete anonymity."

"And you still have that. I just wanted to alleviate the problem by making sure that you really want to keep the donation anonymous."

He considered the terms of Dad's will. He had no choice. "No, you can't reveal who the donor is."

"What if she won't cash the check?"

He drummed his fingers on his thigh. A solution didn't come. If he had access to Daria, if she would confide in him, he could fix this mistake. He frowned. He'd just have to get back with her. How? "She'll cash the check."

Time was all he needed.

"If you're sure, Mr. Vincenzo."

He wasn't, but he had to be. A sigh escaped his lips. "I am." He disconnected, wiped his hands again, then whistled for Spike. The dog had taken to keeping close to the garage. He must have figured out that the garage and apartment were home. No one had answered the ad Paul hung, and part of him was glad.

The dog ran ahead, sniffing and peeing. The dog's favorite place.

He found Jeeves sunning himself by the pool, wearing brightly colored swim trunks. He'd never seen Jeeves so casual. "I need your help."

Jeeves shielded his eyes. "It's my day off."

The pool water lapped against the side. Paul found the sound oddly soothing. "Oh."

Jeeves sighed. "Sit. As long as I don't have to get up, I'll help."

His butt landed on a lounge chair. "I need to get

into Daria's good graces. She won't cash the check unless she finds out who donated the money."

"You can't let her know."

He rubbed a hand down his face. "I realize that. I just need to be close, so she does cash the check."

"What about Spike?"

The dog wandered around the pool trying to drink the water.

"What about him?" Paul glanced at Spike, but nothing jumped out about the dog. He tilted his head and narrowed his eyes at the animal.

Jeeves smirked. "Maybe something is wrong with him."

"Huh?" Then the light bulb blinked on in his head. "I see, and I wouldn't trust his care to anyone else, but her."

He waved a hand at Paul. "There you go. Now hop to it."

"Jeeves, you're a genius. How can I thank you?"

"Bring me some lunch before you call. I have some chicken salad in the fridge. I like mine on whole wheat toast."

Why was Jeeves being so cheeky?

****

Daria sat in her office; her attention was supposed to be on lab results for a terrier mix. The dogs in the back had quieted. The only sound she heard was the tick of the clock. Instead, the large check in an envelope called. Even from the bottom drawer where she'd stashed, she could hear the check.

Leaning back in the leather chair, she stared at the tiles on the ceiling. She could save a lot of dogs with that money. But not if she didn't have the building next door. Maybe she could find a bigger place. She rubbed her eyes and blew out a breath.

Shaking herself, she forced herself to concentrate on what the lab results said. The terrier was already fourteen years old. The blood work indicated the tumor was cancerous. The owner, an elderly lady, would be devastated. This animal was her sole companion.

Her phone rang. She hoped the caller was the lady from United Charities. Instead, her landlord was on the other end of the line. "Joe, do you have good news?"

"As a matter of fact, Vinny's Weenies has decided not to rent the place. The building is all yours."

She sighed. "That's great, Joe. When can we sign the lease?" She had enough for the security deposit and several months' rent. She glanced at the check. The amount would cover the renovations.

If she cashed the darned thing.

With the money, she could offer a lovely place for people to grieve for their pets. She just hated relying on others. Outright charity didn't bother her, but this donation was too suspicious. She didn't trust easily thanks to Mom.

"Let's shoot for next week. I'll call when I know my schedule better."

"Thanks, Joe." She hung up and then stared at the phone. A sigh escaped her lips, and she realized her attention had once again strayed from the paperwork in front of her. Closing the folder, she rubbed her face. "I wish the United Charities lady would call."

Shelley stood in the doorway. She carried in bags of take-out for lunch. "Just cash the check."

Daria cleared the desk, so the two could eat. She unpacked the bag that had been handed to her. "What if this check is drug money?"

Shelley sat. "Do you think an animal really cares where the money for its good comes from?"

Her sandwich sat untouched in front of her. "No, but I do."

"You are too principled."

Daria shook her head. "You cannot be too principled."

"Yes, you can. You won't even cash a check, not for yourself, but for the animals because it could be drug money. Maybe this lady can tell you that the donor is a legitimate business person. Would that information put your mind at rest?"

While she mulled over what Shelley said, Daria took a bite of her roasted vegetable sandwich and chewed. The garlic was subtle enough her mouthwash would take it away. "Why would I believe her?"

"She works for a charitable organization. Why would she lie?"

"Charitable places can be corrupt, too."

"I know, but his place does have a good reputation."

Daria shrugged. She could not make up her mind. Instead, she ate her lunch and contemplated telling someone their dog only had months left.

The phone rang, interrupting her thoughts. Shelley wiped her hands and then answered. She passed the receiver.

"Hello?"

"Daria? It's Paul."

A whole rush of emotions sprouted. She missed him but didn't want to. "Yes, Paul."

"Something's wrong with Spike."
He sounded harried. Her heart went into her throat.

Chapter Twenty-Two

Paul stopped Spike just outside the vet office door. Hunkering down, he held the dog's face. The wind was strong enough to ruffle the dog's short hair. "Spike, I need you to look sick. I wish you could understand me, even if I haven't trained you to do this trick."

Spike licked his face.

He could have sworn the dog understood. Paul narrowed his eyes.

Instead of his happy-go-lucky dog, at a moment's notice, he dropped his tail and padded with his head down.

"Don't overdo the drama, Spike." Paul opened the door to where Daria was waiting. A rush of longing overtook him. He'd missed her. He gripped Spike's leash so hard his knuckles went white. *This had to work.*

She smiled.

He knew she missed him, too.

Then she shifted her focus to Spike. "What happened?"

"He was throwing up again. I think he ate something in the woods around my house."

She shook her head. "You can't let him loose like that."

He hated all of this lying. "But he enjoys the freedom."

She frowned. "You're the human here. You need to do what's best for him."

He accepted the admonishment without comment.

Daria took Spike's leash and then led him to an exam room.

Paul followed, his shoulders slumped. He rubbed the back of his neck.

Spike glanced back.

Daria examined the dog. "He seems okay now, though not his boisterous self. I'd like to keep him and then feed him something in a few hours. If he keeps that food down, he can go home."

"Can I stay?"

She paused, while tapping her chin. "I have a full load of patients, then some people coming in to check out the dogs for adoption."

He smiled. "I can help."

She studied him. "Okay. Don't you have cars to fix?"

"I'm waiting on parts." Paul did have a car to finish, but she didn't need to know. Besides, the car was Gino's, and Gino could use his truck in the meantime.

Shrugging, she put Spike into a cage. "Whatever."

Was he making her uncomfortable?

****

Daria stepped back from the counter.

Paul was standing there. He was in her lab. He was in her office. Her location did not matter. She couldn't breathe in his presence. She'd missed him, despite not wanting to.

Spike returned to the high-energy dog.

He was making her wonder if he'd been sick at all.

Shelley appeared to distract her; each time she thought to confront Paul. An hour after he'd brought in Spike, Daria had her chance. His answer would make or break what would happen next. "Is Spike really sick?"

He stood inches away by the dog's cage. Paul licked his lips, but he never looked away. He tucked his hands into his pockets and slumped his shoulders. "No." He didn't flinch.

She didn't, either. "Then why did you bring him in?"

"Because I had to talk to you."

She didn't know how to respond. No one had ever gone to such lengths to see her. Samuel had always respected her boundaries. Paul didn't notice they existed. "Now you've seen me."

"And I know that you've been doing your best not to be alone with me. What are you afraid of?"

She put her hands into her lab coat pockets. He didn't need to know they were shaking. "I'm not afraid of anything."

He took a step closer, pulling her hands out. "Then why are you trembling? Am I a threat?"

She coughed. "Yes, but not a physical one. You're a threat to my well-ordered life."

A smile creased his face. "That was honest."

She gazed at him with narrowed eyes. "I am always honest."

He put his hands to his heart. "Ouch, Doc. I won't sugarcoat this situation or make excuses. I lied. I'm sorry."

Those two words melted her resolve. She yanked him into a hug. Her body was infused with his warmth. "I missed you as if I'd known you all my life."

"Same here."

His response warmed her, so she let him kiss her, a deep kiss that spoke volumes about his feelings.

Shelley cleared her throat. "Excuse me."

Daria took a step away, but he didn't release her. "What's going on?"

"You have some couples wanting to look at those dogs we rescued."

Paul let her go. "How can I help?"

"Get the dogs while I talk to the couple."

****

As he leashed the large, black dogs in the office's back room, Paul hummed. The smell of bleach tickled his nose. The soles of his shoes squeaked on the tiles.

The other dogs barked.

They licked his face.

He hoped they found a home. His doctor had given him medicine for the allergies which was working. He was surrounded by dogs and not even a sniffle. This situation might work out.

The collars clinked on the sides of the cages. Despite the number of dogs, the place didn't smell like them.

Less than a week ago, he'd never had a dog in his life. Now they surrounded him, because of Daria. He had no idea where this romance would lead, but he vowed to enjoy the ride.

A young couple and their two kids sat in the waiting room.

Daria asked them pointed questions.

The youngest child, a boy of about six, ran to the dogs.

Each dog had a different reaction. One trotted

toward the child. The other hid behind Paul's legs.

He handed the outgoing dog's leash to Daria, intending to put away the other dog.

The woman held up a hand. "Wait. That one is really cute."

He held the dog so the woman could pet him. The kids tried, but the dog shied away.

Paul scratched the dog's head. "Looks like this dog doesn't like children."

"Nonsense," the woman said. "He'll get used to them."

The dog trembled in his arms.

"I don't know about that." Paul glanced at Daria. "I'll put him in the back."

The woman's smile fell off. "But I think he's cuter."

Daria stepped forward. "But the reasons are more than looks. Adopting a dog is also about compatibility. What if your children scare this dog? He could lash out or bite. Then he'd be back here."

The woman squeezed together her lips. "I guess."

He scratched the dog under the chin before putting him back in the cage. He returned to the lobby.

The two kids and the dog were frolicking.

"Looks like the dog picked you."

The husband nodded, but he wasn't smiling. "Let's think about this decision."

The wife frowned. "Harry here doesn't want a dog."

Daria frowned. "The decision should be made by the whole family. I don't want to see him returned because of some behavior your husband doesn't like."

The father raised a hand. "I'm not totally against

the idea. I just think the children are too young."

"Do you expect them to take care of the animal?" Paul asked.

Paul couldn't believe someone thought asking a six-year-old to take care of a dog was a good idea.

"Yes, I was."

"They're too young. If you want them to have a dog, you might want to wait a few years."

The man pursed his lips. "Maybe we'll just do that. Thanks for your time." The man ushered out his family.

The boys glanced back at the dog one more time.

"The kids liked the dogs. Will they be back?" Paul asked.

Daria picked up the Terrier mix, scratching the dog under the chin. "Probably not." She rubbed the dog's nose with hers. "There will be other families, and one of them will be yours."

The dog licked her face.

"We have to name him."

He nodded. He didn't like just calling them the dogs. "How about Snowcap?"

She burst into a smile. "That's great. You'll be Snowcap, then." She took the leash and put him away.

Paul realized he liked being around the dogs.

****

Near the end of that day, Daria settled onto the office chair, and the big check in her drawer called.

Paul was among the missing.

So, she took the paper out, hoping for inspiration. Looking at the zeroes on the face, she imagined what she could do with the money. But only when she found out who sent the money. Who would think that much of her cause to send a large check? She moved her neck, and a crackling noise came out.

"What's that?"

She jumped.

He was leaning on the doorframe, his arms crossed, and a grin on his face.

Should she tell him? Could he help with this decision? "This paper is a check."

He stepped farther into the office, his movements catlike. Taking the paper, he whistled. "That's a lot of kibble."

More than kibble. She tucked some hair behind her ear. It didn't stay, so she undid her messy bun and redid it. "It's kibble and medicine and vaccinations."

Paul watched. "You were looking perplexed."

"I don't know who the donation came from."

He sat on the edge of the desk. "United Charities. Don't they do anonymous donations?"

She leaned back in the chair. He dominated any room he was in. He was a large man, though not as large as Gino. "How do you know about them? Doesn't seem like a mechanic would make an anonymous donation."

He crossed his arms. "I read an article. I understand they check out the donor pretty judiciously. What are you worried about?"

She frowned. "That this donation is drug money."

Paul flinched. "Drug money? You think some guy who sells drugs would be interested in animals?" Paul shrugged. "Lots of people like animals. Why is that so odd?"

"You don't believe the end justifies the means?"

"Not at all."

"This money isn't for you. This donation is for the

animals."

"That's what Shelley keeps saying."

He leaned his forearms onto his thighs. "Then listen. She could be right. Besides, you won't find out who the giver is."

She eyed him. Did Paul know something about United Charities? How could he? "How do you know?"

He shrugged. "Just a guess. If United Charities revealed one name, they'd lose their reputation."

"Okay, then why would someone give anonymously?"

"Who can say how people think? Maybe they won the lottery and don't want people to know."

"Lottery winners are usually on TV. Especially the big ones."

"Then, maybe this person doesn't want any attention. Some people are very private."

She waved her hand. "I could almost buy that if I was curing cancer. As much as I think my work is important, most others don't feel that way."

He leaned forward. "So, you got the one guy who did."

"Why does everyone assume the donor's a guy?"

Paul shrugged. "I do, because I am one."

Daria chuckled. "Fair enough. You want some dinner?"

He cocked his head to one side, a grin on his face. "Don't want to be a bother."

"You couldn't be."

He nodded. "Then, yes, I'll take dinner."

"Oh, I need to shop, then."

He smiled. "Why don't we both shop?"

She couldn't keep the smile off of her face.

Chapter Twenty-Three

Paul realized in the grocery store that Daria never strolled near the meat section. He'd realized she didn't eat meat, but he hadn't known just how strong her aversion was. He cocked his head while pushing the cart.

She waved a hand in the direction of the meat section and shivered. "Just the sight of meat bothers me."

He had to admit, his idea of celebrating was with a good steak. Guess he'd have to rethink this diet. Rethink? Sounded like he was making plans to have Daria in his life for a long time. He'd never thought of anyone that way. "Seeing meat is that horrible?"

"Yes. Is that a problem?"

Paul shook his head. Her being in his life wasn't terrible, nor was he horrified she didn't like meat. "No, not at all." He rubbed her left arm. "Let's get some Portobello mushrooms, and I'll make some burgers out of them."

She smiled.

That smile warmed him.

"That sounds great. You can take Spike home tonight if you want to."

He'd missed his dog. Now today felt like Christmas morning. "I do. I've grown attached to that little critter. I have to say I've never been responsible for anyone or anything in my life." He picked out a few packages of the large mushrooms. He showed them for her approval.

She pushed the cart and nodded. "Shame. Having an animal is such an easy way to teach kids about compassion."

Next, he pointed to the bread section, and he grabbed buns. "Were you surrounded by animals?"

They stood in the checkout line, waiting for their turn before she answered. "I was always bringing home strays to nurse back to health."

He wanted to drink in her peach scent. Something about the fragrance made him dizzy in a good way. "That figures. So, you went into the right profession."

She looked off into the distance for a moment. "Yes, I did. Never wanted anything else."

She had to cash that check. Here was a good time to reinforce the donation. Then his job was done. Not that he was getting out of Daria's life. "You can fulfill your dream even more so with that check." Her puzzled countenance said he might have gone too far.

She tapped her fingers on the cart handle. "Why is that check a big deal?"

"The check isn't. I just want to see your dreams come true." He put a hand to her face. "You've become important."

****

After dinner back at her house, Daria couldn't talk Paul out of washing her dishes.

He'd insisted they could dry in the rack.

But she usually put them away. She was too exhausted to dry. She'd have to face them in the morning or take care of business after he left.

She sipped her wine, leaning on the doorway. She was proud of the place she owned, but it was a dated kitchen. How did Paul see it? "Do you only fix pony cars?"

He rolled up his sleeves and plunged his hands into the soapy water. "I restore them."

After crossing the kitchen, she sat on a chair in the tiny kitchen, watching him. She found a man attractive who wasn't afraid of domestic chores. "Yeah? Any hope for mine?"

He grinned. "Yours could use a lot of work, but the basic structure is solid."

"You've checked the vehicle out thoroughly."

He glanced over his right shoulder. "Yes, I did. Where'd you get it?"

She waved a hand. Because the purchase hadn't been important, she didn't exactly remember. The car had been cheap, and she could drive it off the lot that day. "Some used car dealer."

Paul shook his head. "He had no idea what he had."

She studied him for a moment, wondering what else this man could do. "You aren't just a mechanic?"

He cleared his throat. "No, I'm not."

"How'd you get started on pony cars?"

Smiling, he glanced over his shoulder as he talked. "Dad had one, and when he was getting rid of the car, I begged him for it."

"And the rest is history."

He laughed and put the silverware into the rack. He paused looking at her, leaning his hip against the counter. "So, they say." He wiped his hands and dropped the towel over the drying dishes.

Rising, she crossed the kitchen, scooped up the towel, and hung it on a cupboard door.

But as she did, the towel caught on a dish, and it almost fell.

He grabbed them before the plate broke. "Whoa."

Daria put her hand on her heart. "Oh, Paul. Thank you."

With a mischievous grin on his face, he cocked his head. "You can do better than that."

What was he up to? "Oh?"

He stepped closer, leaning down to be on eye level. "I think my actions deserve a kiss."

She held his head in her hands and let her lips glide over his before taking possession of them. Her heart beat kicked up a notch. His lips were warm as they caressed hers. He tasted of home.

"That's much better. Shall we sit in comfier chairs?" He rested his forehead on hers.

"Sure."

He entwined their fingers, then led her to the couch.

Focusing her attention fully on him, she settled on a chair. "Tell me about your business. Where do you work on cars?"

"In Bernardsville."

The high-end part of this county." She inclined into him. "You have a garage?"

He smiled. "With an apartment above. I had the building constructed."

Cocking her head, she blinked a few times. He wasn't just a poor mechanic, but what else was he? "Oh? Something tells me there is more to you than I think."

"Probably not. Just easygoing Paul."

She studied him for a moment. When did he have time to get work done? "You've spent a lot of time here this week. Don't you have work to do?"

A shrug moved his shoulders. "I'm waiting on parts for the pony car I'm working on now."

She tucked a leg underneath her. "You work on one at a time?"

"I have two bays, but I only like working on one at a time. It's Gino's anyway."

"The car?"

"Yeah. A lot of my business is word of mouth." He looked down at his hands.

She shifted in the chair. "By the way, I never thanked you. He gave me a great price, and he's starting when I need him."

"Good. I'm glad. He's a good guy." Paul smiled.

His grin lit up the room. Daria's curiosity was getting the better of her. She wanted to know everything about him. "He says that about you. How do you know him?"

"Gino and I went to grade school together. He might even be related somehow."

Paul said those words as if family was just a given. Their lives had obviously been different. "Are you from Bernardsville originally?"

"Yes, and I know he doesn't seem like someone from town. He isn't blue blood."

"Neither are you."

"I am sort of."

What exactly did he mean by what he said? She wrinkled her nose, and her voice came out softer. "Really?" She sunk lower into the cushions, yawning, her shoulders slumped.

"I better go. You look bushed."

She was more than bushed.

****

The next day, Daria stood at the bank, rethinking the decision to cash the check. As they walked around her, people's heels clicked on the marble floor. Voices echoed under the tall ceiling.

Paul had advised her to take the money.

Shelley agreed.

This money was for the animals. With four people in front of her, she had too much time to think. She waited for some divine revelation before she did anything else, but nothing in the bank spoke to her.

Tellers counted money, and phones rang.

"You look puzzled."

She'd have never expected Samuel to do something as pedestrian as coming to the bank. "Hello, Samuel. What are you doing here?"

He held up a check, an amused smile on his face. "Just some banking."

She widened her eyes. "I wouldn't expect you to do that at the bank."

He chuckled. "Where else would I do my banking?"

She realized she hadn't made sense. She shook her head. Dressed in jeans and a button-down shirt, he must have taken a rare vacation day. "Online or I assumed you had direct deposit."

"For my paychecks. This one is an expense check."

"Oh."

"So, what are you puzzled about?" he asked.

She looked down at the check, still not sure she

was doing the right thing. She bit her lip. "I received a check from United Charities from an anonymous donor. I'm not sure if I should cash the check before I figure out who donated."

"You won't find out. United Charities is pretty good about discretion."

She leaned closer. "Why would someone want to give something anonymously?"

Samuel shrugged. "Lots of reasons. They might not want the publicity."

She shook her head. "Why not? That makes me think something's wrong with the money."

Samuel straightened. "The check won't bounce."

Daria waved her hands. "I don't expect that. I'm just wondering if someone earned this money illegally."

His grin split his face. "You are the most ethical person I know. In this instance, I think you should think about the end instead of the means."

She was hearing that refrain from everyone. Either they were out of order or she wasn't explaining herself properly to anyone. "That's what Shelley and Paul say."

"Paul. Is that the guy who took you home the other night?"

She searched his face but found no trace of jealousy. "Yes, he did."

"A love interest?"

Her relationship with Paul was not a simple question. What was he? She liked him, and she had the impression that he liked her, too. Shelley would have answered in the affirmative. "Yes, I think so."

He squeezed her right arm. "That's great. Guess I'll have to find a new benefit buddy."

"Sorry, but I'll honor my commitment this

weekend. By the way, you seem to be in a very good mood. Not judgmental at all."

Samuel's grin creased his face. "I met someone."

She couldn't help smiling. If she was happy everyone should be happy, even if she wasn't sure where things were going with Paul. "Good for you."

"Yes, that is good for me. Good for both of us because we aren't consolation prizes anymore."

She put a hand on his arm. *How awful to think that.* "I never thought of you that way."

"But I was safe as long as I was in love with my ex."

She couldn't lie. "I won't deny you being unattainable made things easier. Dating has always been stressful. I enjoyed spending time with you, knowing we could go and just have fun."

He nodded, a warmth in his eyes. "We did, didn't we?"

"More fun than I would have had with anyone else."

Chapter Twenty-Four

As he was just finishing in the garage two days later, Paul answered a call from United Charities. He had been elbow-deep in a pony car that needed a new transmission. If the call had been from anyone else, he would have let it go to voicemail, but he wanted to know when the check was cashed.

He wiped his hands on a rag and then leaned on the car he'd been working on. "This is Paul Vincenzo."

"Hello, Mr. Vincenzo. I'm Laura from United Charities. Just letting you know that your check was cashed."

Paul did a jig. "Thank you for letting me know." After hanging up, he called the main house.

Jeeves answered in his usual droll manner.

"Daria cashed the check." Paul bounced on his toes.

"Then you have your inheritance. I'm proud of you. We should celebrate."

Because Jeeves hadn't been his first thought of whom he wanted to celebrate with, he laughed. "As much as I love you, Jeeves, I plan on celebrating with someone much better looking than you."

"Miss Daria. Shall I cook something?"

He couldn't think of a better way to celebrate. Jeeves could cook anything. "Jeeves, you would be my hero. And I'll give you all the credit.

"Not necessary to give me the credit. I live to serve."

The line disconnected, leaving Paul laughing. He dialed Daria's number with greasy hands. He didn't care. He could clean the phone.

"Happy Valley Veterinary Clinic and Animal Shelter."

He paced around the car he'd been working on his energy at an all-time high. "Hello, Shelley, it's Paul. Could I speak to Daria?"

"Sure. I'll transfer you. How did you talk her into cashing that check?"

"I reminded her the money was for the animals. Maybe she considered me an impartial observer." He didn't think he could take full credit, but he might have exerted a little bit of influence.

"I'm just glad you did. Here she is."

"Paul?"

He stopped and leaned on the side of his garage. When he asked for a date, he didn't need to be out of breath. He wiped his sweaty left palm on his pants. "Hey, Daria, I know I'm calling on short notice, but are you free tonight?"

"I'm not."

"Really? What's going on?" He cringed. Where she was going was none of his business.

"I promised Samuel I'd go to some benefit tonight. This event is the last one I'm attending."

"Okay." His disappointment dripped off his words.

"I'm sorry, Paul. I can't get out of the event, but Samuel and I agreed this fundraiser would be the last one. Wait. He said something about a new love. I'll call and see if he can take her instead."

He straightened. The excitement in her voice warmed Paul. He'd caused that reaction.

"You sure?"

"After this large check, I don't need to beg for money for a while."

"Let me know. I need to jump in the shower, but if I don't answer, then you can leave the message with Jeeves."

"Talk to you later."

Paul climbed into the shower. He hummed some tune playing in his head. He didn't know the words, but right now, those words didn't matter. Tonight, he'd spend the evening with Daria.

Her call lit up his phone.

"Samuel let me go. I'm free tonight."

She sounded excited. He did a dance.

Spike looked at him and rose.

"Let me pick you up."

"I can drive, Paul."

A warmth radiated through him. He had a date tonight. An actual date with just the two of them eating together. "I know, but I want to. You can go home whenever, and Jeeves will be about the place as a chaperon if you don't trust me."

"I don't trust many people, so please don't be offended."

"I'm not. I'll be there in an hour?"

"Okay. See you then."

Paul disconnected and strolled with Spike to the big house. He needed to finalize the details with Jeeves. With a light heart, he bounced into the kitchen.

Jeeves was trolling cookbooks on the kitchen counter. "What did you have in mind for tonight?"

"A vegetarian's delight."

Jeeves widened his eyes. "Vegetarian? I don't think I've ever cooked anything, but meat and potatoes for you."

"Daria eats no meat."

"Oh, that explains everything. I have an idea, and we might have the ingredients."

His date plans complete, he flopped onto a stool. "Jeeves, you are my hero."

"Oh, stop." Jeeves rolled his eyes. "No, don't really."

Paul just laughed, but he hoped Jeeves understood how important this dinner was.

****

Daria didn't know why she remembered at that moment, or why she was in the shower when she did, but she realized one of her patient's owners worked for United Charities. In a conversation with that person was when she had first heard of them. She pushed her face into the hot water. *I just might figure this out.*

Drying off, she calculated she could do her hair, jump into her outfit for the evening, and have enough time to search for the person's number.

With her plan of action secure, she dried and curled her hair, then slid on khaki slacks with a green cotton sweater on top. Satisfied she'd done all she could do to present herself well, she locked the house. She ran across the parking lot. She found the person's folder on the first try. Copying the number, she initially planned to call them tomorrow. Instead, while she waited, she dialed the number. "Mr. Johnson, this is Dr. Daria Jacks. I take care of your dog, Muffin."

"Is everything okay?"

She leaned against the counter in the darkened lobby. "Yes, I need to ask a favor of you."

"Go ahead. You've done so much for Muffin. I couldn't deny you. You remember we adopted Muffin from you in the first place."

Muffin had been hard to place, and when the Johnson family came along and wanted her, she'd rejoiced. "I knew right away you'd be a great family for him." *Am I spreading things on too thick?*

"What's your favor?"

She took a deep breath, leaning her chin on her hand. She rested her right elbow on the counter. "You still work for United Charities?"

"Yes."

"I need to find out who sent me a donation through them."

A sigh came through the phone. "Dr. Jacks, I'm not sure I can honor your request."

She'd thought this request through. "I won't contact them. They don't need to know. I just want to make sure the source is legitimate."

"Did the check bounce?"

She shook her head, knowing he couldn't see her. "No, nothing like that. I just found the situation to be an odd donation."

He sighed again. "I'll do what I can, Dr. Jacks, but I'm not making any promises."

"Thank you, Mr. Johnson." She disconnected.

Paul pulled in, driving the same high-end German car he had the other night.

He'd said the vehicle was his, but how could a mechanic afford such an expensive car?

****

Paul parked by Daria's house but didn't turn off the engine. He got out to open the car door.

A grin split her face.

"What did you just accomplish?" He slid back into the car.

"I could find out who sent that donation."

A chill skittered through Paul, and he felt his stomach drop. If she found out after the fact, would his inheritance be gone? If she did, her knowing could be the end of it all. "Why do you need to know?"

She danced a little in her seat. "I explained that. What if the money is drug money or a pharmaceutical company that tests stuff on animals?"

He struggled to find the right words. She couldn't find out he was the donor. "Those would be bad, I guess. Aren't you just happy to have the money?"

"I still have principles. I can't be bought."

He pinched the bridge on his nose, swallowing hard. "But why are you so sure the money is tainted?"

She put her hands up. "Why else would someone donate anonymously?"

He drove out onto the road, heading to his house. He kept his gaze on the road, but his thoughts were on dissuading Daria. "Maybe they had no choice."

She crossed her arms. "How can you have no choice unless the money is ill-gotten gains?"

He searched for a valid explanation that didn't give up what the truth was. "Maybe the donation is part of entry into some secret society. Or part of a will."

She eyed him. "Who would put a stipulation like that?"

Paul wasn't sure why Dad had put that stipulation in his will, but the reason probably had something to do with how he had lived up until that point. Daria didn't need to know that part. "Someone who wants to control the money from the grave."

"You say that as if you have experience."

He shook his head. "No, but I've heard of things like that." He put his hand on hers. "Let's talk about something else. Before we do, would you think about not pursuing this line of questioning? You don't know what the ramifications will be."

She shook her head. "I'll try, but I'm not sure I can just take the money and run."

He was asking her to do exactly that action. "No one is asking for you to run. Just use the money for what you want. The animals."

She shrugged.

He didn't think he'd convinced her.

"What's for dinner?"

"Steak and—"

"What?" She widened her eyes.

Paul laughed. "Just kidding. No meat."

Daria laughed, too. "I'm sorry to be uptight."

He shook his head. She didn't have to change. "You have your principles. Can't get rid of those."

She shifted to face him, her eyebrows drawn together. "Are you normally a big meat eater?"

He chuckled. At least he'd move the conversation away from the donation. He could breathe a little easier for now. "I'm Italian. Sausage, and things like that, is as much a staple as pasta."

"Oh, sorry."

He gave a curt nod. "No, don't be. I'm seeing a different side of the culinary life."

"Did you cook?"

Another chuckle surfaced. He should have cooked, but he wanted this evening to go smoothly. He was a man who knew how to use his resources, and Jeeves was one of those. "No, Jeeves did. I'm only an average cook. Jeeves is stupendous, though he's never cooked vegetarian. He saw the idea as a challenge."

She frowned. "I'm disrupting your life."

He stopped in front of the big house. The next few minutes were crucial for the future of their relationship. Would she reject him because of his money? Would she care? He held his breath, then let it out. He had to let the chips fall where they might.

She gazed all around the grounds. "Am I disrupting your life?"

Putting a hand on her face, he infused as much warmth into his voice as he possessed. "Yes, because you're the first thing I think about each morning and the last thing each night."

She smiled and blinked. "That was sweet, Paul."

He pointed to the outside. "Shall we?"

She put a hand on the door handle.

"No, wait," Paul said. Let me." He opened her door, smiling down at her.

As she slid out of his car, she looked at the house. She widened her eyes. "Wow. This place is yours?"

"Yes, but the house was given to me by Mom and Dad." Why did he feel the need to add that fact? He had no reason to be embarrassed. He wiped sweaty hands on his pants. The façade with its brick and columns must have captured her gaze. The place screamed old money. Even he knew that situation.

"Given?"

He shrugged. "Yeah, given."

Chapter Twenty-Five

Oh. My. Goodness.

Daria's whole house could fit into Paul's house, twice. She'd never seen a house as large, let alone been in one. She'd been raised in a trailer park.

Even Carmela didn't have a house this big.

Daria's breath caught in her throat. She'd been outclassed on a regular basis at benefits, but this show of wealth took things to a whole new level. What would this guy want?

He put a hand on her back. "The house doesn't bite."

She had to catch her breath before she could move, but she did and stepped in the direction he'd nudged her. Daria couldn't help but smile at Jeeves. He wore black tails. His dark skin seemed even darker than the last time she saw him. "Hello, Jeeves."

He bowed, taking her hand and kissing it. "Good evening, Miss. You're looking lovely."

Paul smacked the side of his head. "I should have complimented her."

Jeeves threw a glance over her shoulder. "You'll have to forgive our Pauly. He forgets his manners sometimes."

The kiss of her hand gave Daria the sensation she was a princess. As her mouth dried, she chewed the inside of her cheek.

"Enough schmoozing, Jeeves. I can take things from here."

Jeeves nodded, closed the door, then disappeared.

He tucked his hands into his pockets. "We can go into the parlor or the front room or the living room."

How was she supposed to make a choice? "Which do you spend time in?"

He cringed. "Honestly I just moved in here again, so I can't say."

"Just moved in?"

He waved a hand. "Long story."

She might want to know that story but another time. She shrugged. "I don't know these rooms, so wherever you want is fine."

"The living room, it is."

He'd put on jeans and a button-down shirt. This date was the first time Daria had seen him in anything but a T-shirt. The shirt he wore had the known logo of a horse and rider.

Leading her down the hall, he shared the stories of some of the portraits on the wall. He pointed to the last one before a doorway. "This portrait was Great Uncle Earl. His father was a bootlegger who married the daughter of a government man."

She studied the portrait. The gilded framed surrounded a man looking off into the distance. Dressed in clothes from one hundred years before, he look elegant. "Did the marriage last?"

He smiled. "Twenty-five years until he was shot in a bar fight."

She smiled along with him. She knew so little of her past, which reminded her that she needed to ask questions at some point. Having no family history hadn't ever bothered her, but seeing how proud Paul was of his made her a little jealous. "You have a colorful past. I know so little about my relatives or ancestors. I've only just reconnected with Mario."

"There's a lot of ancestors."

"Any siblings?" she asked.

He shook his head. "I'm an only, but I have scads of cousins in and around Bernardsville."

She glanced around at the large room they entered. Bookshelves lined on a wall. Floor-to-ceiling windows dominated one end of the room. "I guess this house could fit them all. Where is your shop?"

"At the other end of the estate. I have a separate entrance, but I don't always use that driveway. My friends do."

Estate? She studied the books on the closest shelf. She didn't know much, but she'd bet some of these were first editions. The sheer amount of wealth just in this room staggered her. She turned back. "Did you ever bring Gino up here?"

He shrugged. "Of course. He's a relative somehow." He motioned for her to sit on the brown leather couch.

She did, and the piece of furniture held her like she was valued. Somehow, this home didn't seem like a place Paul lived. He was unpretentious and unaffected by the wealth around him. "Wait. Are you doing this for a reason?"

He settled next to her. "Doing what?"

She waved her hands around. "Showing me all this house. Are you trying to one-up Samuel?"

He narrowed his eyes. "I don't understand."

She swallowed hard, looking at the floor. "You

know that Samuel is rich. I don't choose who I spend time with because of their bank balance."

Paul laughed. He plopped next to her and held his stomach. "No, this house is all real."

Not liking his tone, she pressed her lips together. "Don't make fun."

He took her hand.

His were warm and calloused. The man obviously did a lot of work with his.

Paul cleared his throat. He leaned into her. "I'm not. This house is truly where I live."

She shook her head. "I just don't believe what you're telling me. You're a mechanic."

"I told you I inherited the house."

"Rich kids don't become mechanics."

He softened his gaze. "Poor kids don't become vets?"

"Touché. I'm a little uncomfortable with all this grandeur and subterfuge. None seems real."

She stood.

He stood.

She shuddered, wanting to jump out of her skin. This level of wealth was even beyond Samuel's. This amount was generational wealth, old money as they say which was odd for this part of New Jersey. "Paul, please take me home. I'm disappointed you felt the need for this charade." She marched out the door, but because she could not remember which way she had entered, she paused.

Jeeves appeared with a tray and two wine glasses. "Problem, Miss Daria?"

She let out a nervous giggle. This situation was all too much. She didn't know what to believe anymore.

Whirling, she headed in a direction that might be the way out. When she couldn't figure out where to go, she stopped and glanced back at Jeeves. "I'd like to go. Paul obviously thinks I need to be impressed. I don't and would like to go home. Will you drive me if he won't?"

Jeeves looked from her to Paul, then back. "Uh, Miss?"

Paul held out his hands. "No one is going home. I haven't put on anything for you. I promise. What can I do to prove to you I am who I say I am?"

****

Paul held his breath while he waited for Daria to answer. Fear snaked its way down his spine. A grandfather clock somewhere in the house chimed. He could feel the silence as if it were a living thing. They stood in the foyer. If it had lungs, the curved staircase might have held its breath.

Her face contorted.

He cursed himself for ever portraying himself as anything but what he was. He was rich, and he refused to apologize for having money. For once, he wasn't hiding who he was. He wasn't pretending to be something he wasn't. He'd taken a long time to get to this point, and he wanted her to understand that situation.

Her mouth opened several times, but no words were spoken. Daria finally caught her breath. "Why did you make me think you were poor?"

He tapped his right hand index finger on his thigh. He wasn't sure he could answer that question. He'd assumed some things instead of putting the truth out there. "I never said I was poor. You assumed because I was a mechanic, and I didn't have any money. I've paid my vet bills. I just didn't argue with you. I assumed you wanted a blue-collar guy."

She frowned. "So, you pretended to be one."

He looked around the room, trying to see it from her perspective. "No, I just didn't enlighten you."

She put her hands on her hips, sighing. She looked around, eyes narrowed. "Are you ashamed of who you are?"

Being ashamed wasn't the problem. He'd wanted her so much, that the desire clouded his judgment. Would she understand that idea? He was who he was, and he was finally coming clean. "No, Daria, for once I am not. I won't apologize for having money."

"I'm not asking you to. I just need a minute to adjust. You've lied in the past, and I'm not sure you aren't now."

Spike picked that moment to enter the hall. He wagged his tail and sat at Paul's feet.

"Dogs are usually a good judge of character. And this one picked you."

Spike's vote of confidence bolstered him. He squeezed his hands at his side, and he bounced on his toes. Maybe hope could be found. "Yes, he did."

Jeeves pursed his lips. "Do you even like dogs?"

He gazed at the dog. "I didn't know I did until Spike came along."

Her body turning in on itself, she dropped her shoulders. "I'll stay."

Paul took her into his arms, not wanting to let her go. He kissed the top of her head.

"Glass of wine?" Jeeves asked.

Maybe more than one.

****

As soon as she entered her house, Daria heard her phone ring. The dinner had been magnificent, as had been the company. Jeeves had done a great job making vegetarian fare be highbrow. Even Paul remarked how delicious it was. Her thoughts still buzzed around the idea he was wealthy.

She was intimidated by that fact, but he didn't seem to care. "Hello." Maybe Paul was calling to say goodnight.

"Dr. Jacks. It's Bob Johnson."

"Hello, Mr. Johnson. Do you have news so quick?"

"All I can tell you is the person who donated had to as part of his father's will. Does that make you feel better?"

"Yes and no. Thank you, Mr. Johnson." Daria hung up the phone and sat on the couch to think. "The person might or might not like animals but needed a convenient charity. Why Happy Valley?"

She scratched her head but could not come up with an answer. Dialing Samuel's number, she hoped she wasn't disturbing him. He was a night owl.

"Hello?"

"Samuel, it's Daria. Did I wake you?"

"No, not at all. You should know I rarely sleep."

"I've tracked down some information about my donor. Because of his dad's will, he had to make the donation. You travel in those circles. Can you think of anyone that applies to?"

"Not off hand, but my profession is a small world, and I'll ask around."

Hopefully, Samuel would come up with the answer. If he didn't, she would have to make the decision blind.

****

The day had dawned warm with only a few clouds in the sky. Fixing a car was the last chore Paul wanted to do on such a day. No matter how much he enjoyed what he did, the tug of beautiful days was often hard to resist.

"Pauly, I have something to show you."

Jeeves made a rare trip to Paul's garage. Paul straightened from the engine he was contemplating to see Jeeves with a newspaper. "What's up?"

"You need to see this picture. You know I love Daria…"

He grabbed the paper from Jeeves. In black and white was a picture of her coming out of prison. The caption said she was Mario Loschiavo's illegitimate daughter. He opened his mouth, then closed it. He wasn't sure what to think of this news. "Holy mackerel."

Jeeves took a step towards him. "Have you talked?"

He looked at Jeeves. "No. Do you think I should?"

Jeeves nodded. "She could probably use your support right now."

"True, but doesn't the situation bother you? She looked down her nose at us when she's with the mafia?"

He shook his head. "Her father."

Paul narrowed his eyes. "Her father what?"

"Her father's accused of being with the mafia. I did some research, but she wasn't raised by him. She does have a different last name."

Pauly shook his head, a hint of betrayal coursing

through him. He scratched his arm, mulling over his next move. "I'll have to think about this situation, Jeeves."

"You have nothing to think about. Go to her."

Pauly wanted to trust Jeeves, but he wasn't sure.

Chapter Twenty-Six

Daria decided to visit Mario, after all. To heck with what people think. She'd been bucking trends her whole life trying to fit in, and she had no idea why. The prison no longer scared her, but the smell did make her wrinkle her nose still.

When he entered, his eyes were wide. "I wasn't sure if I would see you again."

She settled on the chair, a fluttering in her chest. "I wasn't sure I was coming here again."

He cocked his head. "What changed your mind?"

She frowned. "Carmela and Maria, my sisters. Odd saying that."

"Oh?"

She took a deep breath. She'd never had family beyond Mom. She didn't look away. "Once they figured out I wasn't after the money, they welcomed me with open arms." She smiled. "I've never had a family before."

He leaned back in the chair. "But what does that have to do with visiting me?"

She gave him some credit and rethought her opinion She'd practiced these words at home. She sat straighter. "You raised them. You raised them single-handedly after their mother died."

He eyed her. "And?"

"That means, despite all this wealth. Despite where

you are now." She gestured toward the surroundings. "You can't be all bad. And maybe…"

"You'll take my money?"

She chuckled. She knew he'd say those words. "No. Not ready to do that. Plus, what would my sisters think of me?"

He smiled and shook his head. "My giving you money doesn't impact them at all. I had a fund put aside just for you."

She opened, then closed her mouth before clearing her throat. "But you didn't know about me."

His face contorted. "I did, sort of. I wasn't sure you were mine."

This situation was more than she could handle. The truth was different than she'd thought about him. "You put money aside, just because?"

"I loved your mother, but she had the same streak you do."

She'd always been compared to Mom. "What streak?"

He looked down at his hands on the table.

They were peasant hands with thick fingers and short-cropped nails.

"That sense of wanting to accomplish things on her own. She could have had an easier life, but she chose not to. I hope you aren't mad at her for that."

"No, I'm not. Never was."

"Good. Now, about that issue you wanted me to figure out."

"You know who my donor is?" She wanted to dance a jig.

****

Paul was finishing Gino's car. He wiped his hands

on a rag, a smile splitting his face when he realized that Daria drove up to his garage.

She climbed out of the car, compressing her lips.

She wasn't happy with him, that he could tell easily. He hadn't known her long, but she wasn't often angry. His smile disappeared. "What's wrong?"

"You're the anonymous donor."

His breath left him for a moment. All of this subterfuge might come crashing down, but maybe it no longer mattered. The inheritance wasn't crucial to his future. "What makes you think that?" He couldn't tell her. Or could he? Nothing stipulated he would be kicked off the estate. He just wouldn't get the inheritance. But where would his business be? He'd wanted some of that money to hire an assistant.

She put her hands on her hips. "Samuel says he heard about the stipulation of your father's will. You told me your father died six months ago."

He did his best to relax his shoulders, but the tension of this conversation settled in them. "He did. I haven't lied, Daria. Calm down."

She frowned. "But you didn't tell me you were the donor."

He sighed, pacing away, then back. "I couldn't."

"Why not?" She crossed her arms.

He rubbed a hand down his face. He hadn't expected her to show up or to have this conversation. "This stipulation was part of the will and was pretty common knowledge. Samuel must have told you that part."

She nodded. "He did."

He'd taken care of all the things he was supposed to do. Even if she didn't care about him, he'd done the right thing. Wasn't thinking outside himself the lesson in Dad's will? He'd thought about someone other than himself. Too bad Daria was being stubborn about the money. "Then what's the problem?"

"I can't take money from a company that kills animals."

Paul sighed. Why didn't the end justify the means? "But, Daria, you can renovate that building any way you want now. You can save many animals."

She took a step back.

Uh-oh.

She studied him. "How do you know about that building?"

He might have stepped in something awful with that comment. Honesty was better, so he just said it. "Gino told me."

She cocked her head, an eyebrow raised. "How do you know I have the building now? The property wasn't available. It would be a..." While she was putting the pieces all together, her voice trailed off. "You. Your Vinny's Weenies. That building was supposed to be a new store."

He'd been happy with his decision. That order was probably his last for the company. "Yes, and I told them to find a new building."

"Why?"

He wanted to shake her and make her see his feelings. "Because, Daria, you wanted that building. You have a contractor, and you now have money. I wanted your dream to come true."

She closed her eyes.

He'd lost her and maybe for good this time. Pain seared through his heart, taking away his breath.

"Why?" Her voice came out as a whisper.

"Why? Why would I do that?"

She snapped open her eyes. "Yes."

"Because, Daria, I'm in love with you."

****

The place was dark, with a carved wood bar running the length of it. The few patrons left them alone. Shelley sat across the table from Daria. "You're an idiot."

Daria had left Paul standing outside his garage, not wanting to hear of love. The whole situation was too much.

Shelley had dragged her to a bar.

The two women sat in a booth, nursing beers.

Daria didn't often drink beer, but today felt as if it was a beer day. "I'm an idiot. Don't sugarcoat your words."

Shelley stared back, her jaw clenched. "I'm not going to. You have this wonderful new family."

Daria rolled her eyes. "Dad's in jail."

She leaned forward. "Looks like he's about to be acquitted."

She waved her hand and took a sip of the bitter beer. "Maria and Carmela are nutty."

"But they've accepted you as you are. You have a trust fund."

She groaned. "Made with dirty money."

Shelley cocked her head. "You insist that is true, but Mario Loschiavo made his money in garbage. And earned the money the honest way, which, once again, I say, will be proven true. And you have this great guy who has gotten you a contractor. And is willing to give you money."

Daria wasn't letting this thought go just yet. She had to be sure about everything before she changed her mind. "From a place that kills animals."

"Okay, yes. You might have that point, Daria, but your troubles are not as big as you think."

She dropped her head on the table, groaning. "Is that why you think I'm an idiot?"

Shelley nodded. "So, give the money back. Let him donate to some other shelter."

She had one more sticking point. This issue she couldn't let go, and she doubted Shelley had any answer to this one. "But his fortune was still made by hotdogs."

Shelley smacked Daria on the side of the head.

Daria held a hand to her head. " Ow. What was that for?"

"You can't ask a guy to give up his kingdom for you."

She blinked and rubbed the spot where she'd been hit. She hadn't realized she was asking him to give up everything. "And I never told him how I feel."

"How do you feel?"

She put her hands on her heart, smiling. "Oh. I love him. I do. I guess I hadn't thought about my feelings."

Shelley looked at the ceiling, then back to Daria. "Shut up or I'll hit you again."

She sipped some more beer. "I want him to give up his kingdom."

"We established that."

She'd treated Paul terribly. Could she make this up to him? "Shelley, I can't ask him to do that."

"Yes, we established that also. What will you do about the situation?"

"I don't know, but I need to fix this."

****

Paul was reminded of when he was a young boy and in trouble. Jeeves had that same stance right now as they stood in the kitchen. He shuffled his feet.

Jeeves studied Paul.

Paul squirmed under the scrutiny.

"Are you sure, Pauly?"

Paul surveyed the big kitchen. He didn't need this much room. "Yes. I'm selling Vinny's Weenies. I'm subdividing this land and selling this house. I only need my garage and my apartment." Jeeves sat at the island like he always did. He had a book in front of him, which was probably something self-help. Jeeves was always looking to improve himself.

Jeeves pursed his lips. "You might not get her back by doing all that."

He took a deep breath, letting the air out noisily. "I know, but these actions feel right. I love what I do, and frankly, I can't run the company anyway."

Jeeves studied him before nodding. "All right, Pauly. I'll stay until the house is sold."

He didn't want Jeeves to stop his life or whatever he had planned. He rubbed a hand down his face. "The subdivision won't be approved right away."

He nodded. "I realize that."

"You don't have to put your plans on hold."

Jeeves put a hand on Paul's arm. "I'm fine."

He looked up at the man who had raised him as much as either of his parents. "What will you do when the house is sold?" His smile lit up the room like a kid at Halloween.

"I'm going south."

He had never seen Jeeves so happy. "Florida?"

Jeeves smirked. "Jersey. South Jersey."

This relative of Jeeves was news. He sat on a stool and waited for the rest of the story. "Jersey?"

Jeeves crossed his arms. "I have a sister who lives in South Jersey."

"Jeeves? You have a family?"

He rose to his full height. "We weren't close, but I've gotten back in touch. Your Daria's father inspired me."

What would he do without Jeeves?

****

Daria awoke the next morning with determination. The headline in the newspaper on her front doorstep reminded her of where she should have been yesterday, which was in court with her family. She called Carmela.

"Oh, Daria, you've heard. I tried to call you."

Her focus had been elsewhere. "My cell battery died."

"No problem. He's free. That's all that matters. The prosecutor apologized. Now everyone can see Dad isn't a criminal."

"Even me."

"Oh, you didn't know him. It was a likely conclusion to jump to. Dad forgives you. Which means, you have to come over for a celebration."

Daria needed to know something else. "Carmela?"

"Yes."

This question was crass, but they were family, right? "How did he make his money?"

Carmela laughed. "In the trash business. Really, he did."

She couldn't resist asking the obvious question. Since Dad had been exonerated, this thought had plagued her. "Why did he let me believe he was a crook?"

"Because he wanted you to come to your own conclusions. He wanted you to figure out his situation on your own. Besides, he was in jail. Would you have believed him?"

"Probably not. What time is the celebration?"

Carmela squealed. "You'll come?"

"I wouldn't miss the event for the world." Daria had one more thing to do today, so she ended up on Paul's doorstep.

Jeeves opened the door.

"Jeeves? What's the *For Sale* sign doing on the lawn?" *If Paul sells the house, will I ever see him again?*

"Your Pauly is selling the house."

"Isn't his garage on the property?"

Jeeves jammed his hands into his pockets. "Maybe you should speak to him directly."

"Is he down at the shop already?"

"Yes."

Since the weather was nice, and Daria had lots of nervous energy, she rambled to the garage.

Spike lay outside in the sun. When he saw her, he barked.

"What do you see, Spike? Rabbit?" Paul poked his head around the wall. He stepped completely out of his garage.

He looks good. She stopped, her heart fluttering. "Hi." *Brilliant!*

"Hi to you."

She crossed her arms. "Uh, selling the place?"

He wiped his hands on a rag. "Yes. This place isn't me. I'm hoping I can subdivide the lot and keep my garage here."

So he wasn't moving away. This would give her a chance to make it up to him. "I see."

Spike settled at her feet.

"How's Spike doing?" she asked.

Paul puffed out his chest. "I have him in obedience class. He's getting all *A*s."

"Good to hear."

He leaned against the side of the garage, his arms crossed. "You didn't come here to talk about Spike."

She licked her lips. "No, I didn't." She let out a breath. "I don't want you to sell."

"The house or the business?" He blinked.

This situation was worse than she thought. She'd broken this man's heart so badly, he was changing his entire life. "You're selling the business?"

"Vinny's Weenies is for sale. I can't run the company."

I am too late. "Don't."

Paul shook his head. "I've made up my mind."

She'd messed up this relationship, and now she couldn't fix it. "Don't do the selling for me."

He flashed a wry grin. "I'm not actually selling for you. I don't need the house. I don't need the land. I don't even need the income from the business. I'm doing fine on my own."

That is good to know. "Oh?"

He put his arms out to his sides. "I make a good living with my automobile refurbishment business. I can support myself all on my own."

She pondered his words for a moment. "You don't want to be rich?"

He laughed. "I didn't say that."

"Huh?"

He shook his head. "I'm rich on my own, Daria. My business is booming. I don't need Dad's fortune. I learned a little self-reliance from you."

This conversation was laying her soul bare. "I asked you to give up your kingdom, so I came back to tell you not to."

Paul chuckled. "This house and property weren't my kingdom." He waved at the garage. "This is my kingdom."

She surveyed the place. The space looked cleaner than she would have expected a garage to be. All the tools were hung up. The floor was a shiny white. The only dirt was on the rag that Paul held. She turned back. "Still, I'm sorry."

A frown creased his face. "For what? Helping me see I don't need Dad's money?"

She put a hand on her heart. That organ was beating faster than normal. *She helped him.* "Did I do that?"

Paul stared at his fingers. "Yes, you did. And no matter how you feel about me, I'm grateful you did that."

Now was the time. In fact, if she didn't share her feelings, she might never have the courage. "Uh, about how I feel." She wasn't sure if she should get closer. She might have stomped on his heart too hard. He might not forgive her for hurting him. He reminded her of a puppy waiting for a treat.

He turned to face her full-on. He even leaned a

little bit closer. "Yeah?"

She licked her dry lips and swallowed even if her mouth was dry. Should she just say it? Her mother used to tell her to just get over with it. "Well, I guess, now I know. Oh, Paul, I love you."

She held her breath as the silence lengthened between them. He wasn't giving away his emotions. She wanted to shake him so he would say something. The silence stretched to what seemed like an eternity,

He whooped. Then he ran and spun her around. Setting her on the ground, he gave her a tender kiss. "I'm so glad." He let go.

She was still a little dizzy, and she had to sit on the grass. This relationship was really happening. This girl from the wrong side of the tracks had fallen in love with a rich man. And he loved her back.

He hunkered down in front of her, his arms resting on his thighs. "You okay, Daria?"

She flashed him a big smile as she stared into those eyes that didn't care if she didn't have enough hair color to cover her white trash roots. He'd said he loved her. "Couldn't be better."

She loved this man and he loved her.

A word about the author...

Chris Redding is a graduate of Penn State and a diehard Nittany Lions fan. She's lived in three states and three countries, but now calls West Virginia home. She's been a writer since she was ten and has written or ghostwritten sixty novels and novellas.

http://www.chrisreddingauthor.com

Thank you for purchasing
this publication of The Wild Rose Press, Inc.

For questions or more information
contact us at
info@thewildrosepress.com.

The Wild Rose Press, Inc.
www.thewildrosepress.com